NO GUTS, NO GLORY

Whereas white men usually lunged in for a deep thrust into vitals, Indians preferred a fast, furious slashing attack, cutting their opponent to ribbons and bleeding the fight out of them.

That's exactly what this one had in mind now. He danced left and right, slashing rapidly with his knife as he edged in closer, trying to unnerve this buckskin-clad white man. At one point he surprised Fargo by leaping forward enough to slash Fargo's chest. Luckily, the thick buckskin shirt took most of it and Fargo felt only a brief lick of hot pain.

Fargo feinted left, then spun around rapidly on one heel and slashed the brave's left shoulder deep. He suddenly dropped onto his ass and put his long legs to good use, wrapping them around the Indian's knees and rolling over hard to bring him down. In an eyeblink Fargo was on him, driving the toothpick deep into his abdomen—so deep that Fargo felt the rush of heat on his hand as the brave's vitality escaped.

D1013506

THE TRAILSMAN

#364

ROCKY MOUNTAIN RUCKUS

by

Jon Sharpe

A SIGNET BOOK

SIGNET
Published by New American Library, a division of
Penguin Group (USA) Inc., 375 Hudson Street,
New York, New York 10014, USA
Penguin Group (Canada), 90 Eglinton Avenue East, Suite 700, Toronto,
Ontario M4P 2Y3, Canada (a division of Pearson Penguin Canada Inc.)
Penguin Books Ltd., 80 Strand, London WC2R 0RL, England
Penguin Ireland, 25 St. Stephen's Green, Dublin 2,
Ireland (a division of Penguin Books Ltd.)
Penguin Group (Australia), 250 Camberwell Road, Camberwell, Victoria 3124,
Australia (a division of Pearson Australia Group Pty. Ltd.)
Penguin Books India Pvt. Ltd., 11 Community Centre, Panchsheel Park,
New Delhi - 110 017, India
Penguin Group (NZ), 67 Apollo Drive, Rosedale, Auckland 0632,
New Zealand (a division of Pearson New Zealand Ltd.)
Penguin Books (South Africa) (Pty.) Ltd., 24 Sturdee Avenue,
Rosebank, Johannesburg 2196, South Africa

Penguin Books Ltd., Registered Offices:
80 Strand, London WC2R 0RL, England

First published by Signet, an imprint of New American Library,
a division of Penguin Group (USA) Inc.

First Printing, February 2012
10 9 8 7 6 5 4 3 2 1

The first chapter of this book previously appeared in *Death Devil*, the three hundred
sixty-third volume in this series.

The Trailsman

Beginnings . . . they bend the tree and they mark the man. Skye Fargo was born when he was eighteen. Terror was his midwife, vengeance his first cry. Killing spawned Skye Fargo, ruthless, cold-blooded murder. Out of the acrid smoke of gunpowder still hanging in the air, he rose, cried out a promise never forgotten.

The Trailsman they began to call him all across the West: searcher, scout, hunter, the man who could see where others only looked, his skills for hire but not his soul, the man who lived each day to the fullest, yet trailed each tomorrow. Skye Fargo, the Trailsman, the seeker who could take the wildness of a land and the wanting of a woman and make them his own.

*Montana (Northern Nebraska Territory),
1860—where Death takes the pleasing
form of three beautiful sisters
with a secret.*

1

"Fargo, I got a God-fear that somebody is following us," said Captain Jasper Dundee.

Skye Fargo, riding out ahead on the rock-strewn mountain trail, nodded. He was a tall man clad in buckskins, wide in the shoulders and narrow in the hips. "Been following us for the better part of two hours, I'd reckon."

Dundee, a weathered campaign veteran of the U.S. Cavalry's Department of Dakota, slewed around in the saddle to study their back trail. "Redskins, you think?"

Fargo shook his head. "You know how it is with the red aborigines, Jasp. When they take a notion to follow you, you won't know it until you hear the war whoop. No, these are white men."

"That rings right to me, Trailsman. And seeing's how white men are scarce as hen's teeth this high up, it's a good chance these slinking coyotes are Dub Kreeger and his gang of deserters. Might even have their sights notched on us right now."

Fargo whipped the dust from his hat and twisted around to grin at the officer. "Could be. Let's hope army marksmanship training is as piss-poor as I believe it is."

Fargo faced front again, his eyes crimped to slits in the brilliant spun-gold sunshine of a summer day in the Rocky Mountains. Some of the fringes on his faded buckskins were crusted with old blood. His crop-bearded face was half in shadow under the broad brim of a white plainsman's hat.

The breathtaking view out ahead of them was familiar to Fargo, but he always gazed upon it as if seeing it for the first time. Many back in the States still believed the Rocky Mountains were a single wall rather than a series of parallel ranges. He could see them clearly now like ascending curtain folds, with the cloud-nestled spires of the imposing Bitterroot Range forming the final great barrier to human exploration.

"Think we'll ever tame 'em?" Dundee called out behind him. "These mountains, I mean."

Fargo mulled that one. Two decades earlier Hudson's Bay Company men had swarmed this region until driven out by Nathaniel Wyeth's Rocky Mountain Fur Company. But the London dandies no longer craved beaver hats, and now the region was mostly populated by Indians, silver and gold miners, soldiers, and a few hearty independent trappers. Fargo considered this land bordering the rugged Canadian Rockies one of the most pristine and spectacular places in the West—but also in grave danger of being overrun by "cussed syphillization."

"Tame them, no," he finally replied. "Leastways I hope not. But unless the New York land hunters and the rest of them nickel-chasing fools back east are reined in, these mountains will be blasted into slag heaps by the miners and railroad barons."

"Spoken like a true bunch-quitter," Dundee said.

Something glinted from the slope above the pass.

"See that?" Dundee called forward.

Fargo nodded. "That wasn't quartz or mica, not this far up. Hell, our horses are blowing hard even at a walk. Knock your riding thong off, Jasp, and break out your carbine—we might have a set-to coming."

"Suits me right down to the ground. I'd admire to ventilate Dub Kreeger's skull. I knew that crooked bastard back at Fort Robinson. Just another scheming snowbird—joined the army in fall to get out of the cold, then lit out at the first spring thaw. Only, he liberated three hundred dollars from the Widows and Orphans Fund before he and his greasy bootlicks left."

"I heard he got himself arrested in the Black Hills?"

"That's the straight," Dundee confirmed. "All four of 'em were in the stockade. They shoulda danced on air long ago. But they killed two guards and pulled a bust out. Made off with two cases of ammo, too. Lately they've taken to this high country and raiding on the new Overland route between South Pass and the Oregon Territory."

Dundee paused to survey the slopes around them. "Damn fool idea, Fargo, this new Overland route."

"Sure it is. But it was also a damn fool idea for the army to build the road that made it possible. All it did was stir up the featherheads."

"That's exactly what I told Colonel Halfpenny. There's no civilian law up here and damn few soldiers. Now there's three way-station men murdered, two Overland teamsters missing, a payroll missing, and God knows what happened to the three widows. And to cap the climax, Flathead Indian attacks have closed off the route and marooned Robert's Station."

"Oh, there's law up here," Fargo gainsaid. "Gun law. But I'm with you on all the rest. And sending one soldier into these mountains is dicey enough, if you take my drift."

Dundee took it, all right. He and Fargo had been sent out of Fort Seeley to investigate the apparent heist of an army payroll as well as the fate of missing civilians. Seeley was a small garrison meant to protect prospectors in the Bitterroot Range. But a troop movement this high into the mountains could ignite a full-blown Indian war, especially with the Flathead tribe whose clan circles dotted this region.

Fargo's Ovaro flicked its ears several times. Since there were no flies at this altitude, Fargo read it as a warning the stallion was picking up sounds—sounds that didn't naturally belong to the area.

"Trouble's on the spit," he told Dundee. "But since they're up above us, there's no point in holing up. We'd be fish in a barrel. Our smartest play is to keep them back out of range until we hit the new federal road, then outrun 'em. Break out your spyglasses and glom that slope good."

"If it's the Kreeger bunch," Dundee opined as he pulled out his brass field glasses, "they'll likely have their stolen army Spencers. It's a good weapon at the short and middle distances, but that short barrel makes it unreliable over three hundred yards."

Several minutes passed in silence, the only sounds the hoof clops of their mounts and the occasional moaning of wind funneling through the pass. But Fargo felt the presence of imminent danger, as real as the man beside him.

"You know anything about these three widows?" Fargo asked.

Dundee chuckled. "I wondered when you'd get around to them, Lothario. No, I don't know much. But all three are sisters, and my hand to God, they were married to three brothers."

"Ever meet these brothers?"

"Nope. According to our records, they were named Stanton—Cort, Lemuel, and Addison Stanton. Hardworking and honest according to Overland."

"How do you know for sure they were killed?"

"An express rider found the bodies, all shot in the head. Sounds like the payroll coach showed up at the station minus the driver and messenger guard. These three fellows went out to see if they could find the missing men."

Fargo nodded. "Well, last I heard the Flathead tribe has very few barking irons. Besides, they like to take prisoners alive and bring them back to the village for torture. If a prisoner acts tough and stands up to it good, they'll generally let him go."

"Mighty white of 'em," Dundee said sarcastically.

"More than you'll get from an Apache or Comanche, soldier blue. So what about the strongbox?"

"Yeah, what about it? I agree with you that white men likely killed those teamsters, and that almost surely means Dub Kreeger and his two-legged roaches. I s'pose they got it."

"I don't," Fargo said flatly. "Not if that's the Kreeger gang watching us right now."

Dundee, still watching through his glasses, let that remark sink in for a minute. "Yeah, all right, you've got a good point and I'm caught upon it. If that pack of yellow curs laid their paws on twenty-eight thousand dollars, why in blue blazes would they still be in this area, right? Sure as cats fighting they'd be on their way to San Francisco or Santa Fe."

Fargo nodded. "So either they didn't get it or that's not them getting set to perforate our livers."

"Fargo, you've got a poetical way of speaking," Dundee said sarcastically.

Again the Ovaro pricked his ears, but this time Fargo wasn't so sure it was a danger sign—his own frontier-honed ears picked up faint sounds from the right side of the trail. Sounds remarkably like feminine laughter.

"Jasp," he called out, "light down and hobble your mount. Bring your spyglasses, too."

"Trouble?"

"Most likely—sounds like females."

Both men swung down, tied their horses foreleg to rear with rawhide strips, then wormed their way through the boulders massed along the trail. A minute later they emerged onto a large traprock shelf overlooking a small valley with a white-water stream churning through it.

Dundee stared, jaw slacked in astonishment, then brought his field glasses up for a better look. Fargo followed suit.

"Son of a splayfooted bitch," Dundee said in a reverent whisper. "Are you seeing the same thing I am, Fargo?"

"Yeah. We can't both be dreaming."

Below, in the center of the verdant valley, the noisy stream crashed over a rock lip, forming a small waterfall and a natural pool. Three young women, shapely, pretty, and naked as jaybirds, frolicked in the pool.

Fargo said, "There's our three widows, I'd wager. Don't appear to be mourning, either."

"Well, keep up the strut! Two gorgeous brunettes and a blonde who looks like the youngest," Dundee said. "The only place I've seen tits like that is on those French playing cards."

"These ain't psalm singers neither," Fargo said, glancing at the formidable cache of weapons at the edge of the pool. "These three nymphs are loaded for bear."

"A woman should be well-heeled up in these mountains, Trailsman."

"Actually, a woman shouldn't be up here at all."

However, Fargo's words lacked all conviction as he watched one of the brunettes bend over to scrub her legs.

"Look at that, won'tcha?" Dundee said in a voice gone raspy with lust. "That sweet, firm ass baying at the moon.

And look! The blonde is sudsing her tits! Jesus, Fargo, maybe we'll roll a seven, huh? They got no men now."

"We're ordered to bring them down out of the mountains, Jasp, not to bed them."

Still staring through his glasses, Captain Dundee made a farting noise with his lips. "You sanctimonious hypocrite! Christ, every morning you have to comb the pussy hair out of your teeth. You telling me you don't plan to tap into that stuff?"

Fargo grinned. "I'm a man likes a challenge, so I aim to hop on all three of 'em. Then I'll trim each one separately."

Dundee laughed. "I'm ugly and going bald, so I'll settle for just one. Maybe—"

Dundee never got his next word out. Fargo heard a sickening sound like a hammer hitting a watermelon followed a fractional second later by the reverberating crack of a cavalry carbine. The back of Dundee's head exploded in a scarlet blossom, and the officer folded to the ground like an empty sack.

2

At the sound of the gunshot all three women grabbed their weapons and clothing and headed north across the valley. Fargo covered down behind a boulder and worked out the bullet's trajectory, following it back to its source, worried about the horses. Putting a man afoot in this high country was a death sentence.

The bullet had entered the back of Dundee's skull high and plowed its way downward, exiting beside his nose. Fargo calculated that that placed the shooter about halfway up the steep southern slope—a fancy piece of shooting, he admitted with a twinge of guilt. Distracted by those three naked beauties below, he and Jasper had gotten careless.

He had no idea if the shooters were sticking, but after a careful reconnoiter Fargo was certain he knew the position they'd used: a nest of rocks in a pocket of deep shadow. The horses appeared to be at too steep an angle below them for the ambushers to kill. Fargo crawled out to the trail, eased his 16-shot Henry from the scabbard, and jacked a round into the chamber.

His face quietly dangerous, he scuttled backward, crab fashion, to improve his line of fire. Then he threw the brass-framed repeater's butt plate into his shoulder socket, drew a bead on the nest, and opened fire. The Henry bucked into his shoulder rapidly as he levered and fired. Fargo didn't let up, levering rapidly, brass shell casings clattering to the rocks all around him until he had emptied the tube magazine.

His marksmanship took good effect—he watched men boil out of the nest and run over the crest of the slope. Four of them.

"Dub Kreeger and his greasy shit stains," Fargo muttered, his face hot with sudden anger. "We'll be huggin', boys, that's a fact." It was now Fargo's obligation, by a code as old as Hammurabi, to balance the ledger for this murder.

Fargo now faced an unpleasant task. He unlashed the entrenching tool from Dundee's saddle and, after clearing away some surface rocks, dug a grave in the flinty soil beside the narrow trail. He tugged the officer's body over to it and laid him to rest. After shoveling the dirt back in, he removed a flask of gunpowder from one of Dundee's saddle pockets.

How many times, Fargo wondered as he spread the gunpowder over the new grave, had Captain Jasper Dundee done this for his fallen comrades? Fargo pulled a lucifer from his possibles bag, thumb-scratched it to life, and flipped it on the gunpowder. The stench would linger and chase off any carrion animals.

As the powder sparked and fizzled, Fargo removed his hat. "I ain't got the words, Jasper," he apologized in a quiet mutter. "You know I wasn't Bible-raised, and heathens are poor shakes at praying. You were a credit to your dam, a good man to ride the river with, and you had more guts than a smokehouse. You know that my word is my bond, and I will carry out this mission we were charged with. And soon enough it'll be turnabout—come hell or high water, I aim to plant every one of those jackals who doused your light."

Fargo clapped his hat back on, tossed the soldier a final salute, then tied the sorrel to the Ovaro's bit with a lead line. He forked leather and gigged the Ovaro forward, constantly scanning the slope on his left in case Kreeger's gang decided to return and finish the job.

"Stay sharp, old warhorse," he told the Ovaro, patting his neck. "You're always the first one to know."

Fargo and Dundee had chosen to avoid the new federal road because of the local Indian uprising. According to Fargo's army map, Robert's Station was four miles from the spot of Dundee's murder, sticking to this trail. But as the crow flies across the valley where the women bathed, Fargo figured it was only about a mile. He could not, however, risk laming the Ovaro to descend the steep, rocky slope.

The sun was shining dully straight overhead when Fargo rounded the shoulder of the mountain and the station hove into view. He saw immediately that it was a good defensive position. The sturdy structure of notched logs with a shake roof had no windows and was loopholed for rifles. The leather-hinged slab door was reinforced with iron bands.

Fargo hauled back on the reins, pausing to study the station closer. There was a small, hoof-trampled pole corral and a stock barn with a stone water trough in front of it. An abandoned Overland coach sat beside the barn. Fargo spotted neither man nor beast.

"Hallo, the station!" Fargo sang out. "Skye Fargo riding in under orders from Fort Seeley!"

Ominous silence greeted his announcement. Fargo shrugged and nudged his stallion into motion. He had progressed perhaps fifty feet when a rifle spoke its piece and his hat went spinning off his head. Fargo had the reflexes of a cat and caught it in one hand before it hit the ground.

"Nice catch, mister!" called out a musical female voice. "But the next thing to fly off will be your head! Just rein that handsome horse around and reverse your dust."

"Nice shooting, too," Fargo replied. "But I can't do that, lady. And you've no call to get on the peck. The army sent me up here to help you folks get out—and to find out what happened to that missing payroll."

"Uh-huh, I'm sure that strongbox is on your mind, all right. Mister, you say the army sent you, but you sure's hell ain't no soldier. Now skedaddle. Nobody asked you to stick your nose in the pie. I'd hate to kill a man as handsome as you."

"'Preciate the compliment, ma'am. Makes up for this new hole in my conk cover. There was a soldier with me— Captain Jasper Dundee from Fort Seeley. But he was murdered this morning by Dub Kreeger and his gang. That's his cavalry sorrel I'm leading. You must've heard the shot—you and your sisters took off like spooked antelopes."

This announcement was greeted by a long silence while Fargo listened to the breeze sough in the few scraggly pine trees clinging this high.

"You mean you was watching while we . . . ?"

"Only a fool or a liar," Fargo admitted, "would say he didn't watch. How often does a man get to gaze on paradise while he's still mortal?"

Fargo heard female tittering greet this remark.

"Oh, you're a silver-tongued one, all right. Well then, ride in slow. But no parlor tricks, stranger, hear? There's three weapons trained on you, and might be we're only women but we all know how to shoot plumb."

Fargo let the Ovaro walk in slow, keeping his gun hand out wide. He swung down, hobbled both mounts, and thumped on the door. It swung open quick and the first thing he noticed was the business end of a double-barreled express gun. The next thing he noticed was the gal holding it on him— the succulent young blonde he had seen bathing earlier.

"Take his gun, Sharlene," ordered the voice that had been talking to Fargo. "And fetch that Arkansas toothpick outta his boot—he sizes up as the kind of man who knows how to use it."

"Well now, ladies," Fargo quipped, "this is shaping up to be some kind of 'rescue mission,' all right. But who's going to save me?"

Sharlene, one of the two shapely brunettes, tugged Fargo's Colt from its holster, batting big, wing-shaped, emerald eyes at him. Her full, heart-shaped lips were luscious as ripe cherries and Fargo suddenly had an appetite for fresh fruit.

"What's your name again?" the other brunette, armed with a Volcanic repeating rifle, demanded.

He glanced around the big room. A long trestle table for the passengers' meals and a potbelly stove made up most of the scant furnishings. "Skye Fargo, ma'am," he replied.

Her pretty face looked skeptical. "Sounds made up. Is that your name *this* summer?"

"Say, hold up, Darlene," the blonde interjected. "Skye Fargo . . . he's the hombre your Cort read to us about—you recall, from that *Frontier Sagas* magazine he use to like?"

"Why, Marlene's right!" Sharlene exclaimed. "The buckskins, the boot knife, the beard and lake blue eyes . . . he's the very man!"

"Darlene, Sharlene, and Marlene?" Fargo repeated, politely amused.

"Our folks wasn't too imaginative," Darlene explained. "I'm the oldest, Sharlene is the middle sister, and Marlene is the baby."

Fargo's eyes raked over the curvaceous blonde. "Mmm . . . just an infant."

Darlene wagged the barrel of her Volcanic. "Just keep it in your pocket, Mr. Skye Fargo. She's a new widow—we all are. Don't matter to me how many ink slingers talk you up big. Don't get any big ideas just because you seen us naked."

Fargo tugged at his beard, mulling things. "Well, this area is crawling with warpath Indians. And Overland has permanently closed this line. You'll have to leave, you know."

"We know," Darlene said evasively, exchanging a quick warning glance with both of her sisters. "But we ain't ready to go just yet."

Fargo did a double take. "Not ready—? Lady, this isn't Fiddlers' Green. You're caught between a sawmill and a shoot-out. I take it Dub Kreeger has already sent in his card?"

"We can handle that polecat," Darlene said. "Same with the Indians."

"And anyhow," Sharlene chimed in, "the Indians been layin' low since they saw us bury our husbands."

"That won't last long," Fargo explained. "They're superstitious about going near a place where somebody just died. They believe a dead man's soul hovers near his burial place and jumps into the first new body who gets close enough. Believe me, the grace period is short. They'll be on this place like ugly on a buzzard."

Darlene's face set itself in defiant lines. "You aim to force us outta here, Fargo?"

"I don't *force* women to do anything," Fargo said, "even when they're unarmed."

Darlene finally lowered the weapon. "I believe that much. You don't strike me as the kind who has much trouble convincing women."

"If you ladies don't mind my asking, why in the hell do you want to remain here? You're cut off from resupply and you must be low on eats. There's not that much game this high up."

"Plenty of fish," Marlene said. "Bass and trout. Now and again we plink a rabbit. And Crazy Charlie fetches serviceberries and wild onions and such."

"Crazy Charlie?"

"Charlie Waites," Darlene explained. "He's been the stock tender since Robert's Station opened. He's prob'ly sleeping one off in the barn right now. He's priddy much a useless drunk who spends all of his time trying to see us girls naked. Makes out like he's crazy, but I don't credit his act. It just gets him out of work. We keep him around, though, on account he's a fair shot with a rifle. Knows how to scare off Indians, too."

Fargo nodded. "All that's good to know, but you still haven't answered my question. Why are you sticking around here when it's so dangerous?"

Darlene suddenly assumed a pious face. "We just buried our husbands, that's why. We ain't ready to desert them."

Fargo might have believed that foolish, sentimental claptrap if another woman had given it. But he suspected Darlene was about as sentimental as a landlord.

"I ask," he said cautiously, "because there's good reason to believe that Dub Kreeger's bunch don't have that strongbox. Indians are lazy and wouldn't bother hauling it around if they couldn't see the use of it."

"And so you're hinting around that we got it?"

"No, ma'am. It's just a mite curious. I'm under orders to bring you ladies *and* that twenty-eight thousand dollars back to Fort Seeley. I'm sure all three of you know that money is not finder's keepers—it belongs to Uncle Whiskers."

"That coach rolled in here empty," Darlene insisted, "and the strongbox was gone. That's all we know."

Fargo nodded. "All right. But I'm under orders to find out all I can about it. And if you ladies aren't quite ready to pull up stakes, I reckon I'll have to wait around until you are."

"Suits me," Marlene and Sharlene said in chorus, but Darlene shot them a dark scowl.

"I admit having a frontier hero around is comforting. But you ain't staying in this station house," she informed Fargo bluntly.

Again Fargo nodded. "Didn't expect to, ma'am."

"But you'd like to, wouldn't you?" she taunted.

Fargo eyed the Volcanic and then the express gun. "Well,

it could be mighty pleasant—but also a mite deadly. I'll try not to close herd on you."

Fargo stepped outside to tend to the horses. First, though, he walked around the pole corral to have a look at the coach.

It was riddled with bullet holes, and tacky blood spotted the box where the driver and shotgun messenger had ridden. But there were also a half dozen arrows, fletched with crow feathers and tipped with sharpened flint, protruding from the coach. Fargo refused to believe that the Flathead tribe joined forces with Kreeger's gang—the untamed tribes in these mountains would rather deal with the yellow vomit than whiteskins.

Which might mean, Fargo surmised, that Kreeger's gang attacked the coach and were interrupted by Indians on the scrap. Retreat would have been the wise course, and perhaps that retreat was forced before they could lay hands on the strongbox. But if so, where was it? Indians would not have troubled with something that heavy nor could they possibly open it. It was just possible that the stagecoach rolled into Robert's Station with the payroll still on it . . .

Darlene's voice drifted back to him: *We just buried our husbands. We ain't ready to desert them.*

"Ain't that tender?" Fargo muttered. "Widows pining over the graves."

Fargo warned himself not to be lulled by their beauty—if these three were the "gentle sex" he was the Roman Pope. Fargo untied the hobbles and led the Ovaro and Dundee's big cavalry sorrel into the pole corral. He stripped off the leather and gave both horses a quick, brisk rubdown with an old gunnysack. Then, after watering them at the stone trough, he fed each one oats from his hat.

"Gotcha!" a shrill voice suddenly shouted from behind him and Fargo tucked and rolled, clawing for his Colt.

3

Fargo rolled several times, hard, then came up on his knees ready to fan his hammer. But instead of a vicious killer looking to burn him down, he spotted a slight, homely, unarmed man with a moon face and stiff red hair like a wire brush. The man aimed his index finger at Fargo, cocked his thumb, and said, "Bang!" Then he giggled like a schoolboy.

Fargo, shaking his head in disgust, leathered his shooter and pushed to his feet. "You're Crazy Charlie, I take it?"

"Take it, shake it, but don't break it—took my mama nine months to make it!"

This sent the moon-faced man into a new paroxysm of giggles.

"You're a caution, all right," Fargo said sarcastically. "You damn near got yourself killed, funny man. My name's Fargo, by the way."

"I'm not funny, Fargo, I'm crazy. A crazy son of a bitch as mad as a March hare. The redskins won't touch me—afraid to. I'm heap bad medicine."

Fargo trained a skeptical gaze on him. "Most madmen don't believe they're crazy."

"See there? That's how consarn crazy I am. Too loco to even hide it."

The self-proclaimed madman threw back his head and howled like a timber wolf. "Most men won't eat pussy, but *I* will!"

"That ain't crazy. Just a matter of . . . taste."

Fargo turned his head in disgust until Crazy Charlie was done digging in his nose with an index finger.

"Charlie," Fargo said, "you're the stock tender—what do you know about this Overland coach?"

Crazy Charlie studied it for a full minute, pulling thoughtfully at his chin.

"I believe it has four wheels," he finally announced. "Yes, I'm sure of it."

Fargo twirled his Colt out of the holster and thumb-cocked it, aiming center of mass at the supposed lunatic. "Could be you didn't hear me. I said what do you know about this Overland coach?"

Suddenly he looked less crazy. "It's a Lancaster County coach, Pennsylvania. Made by the Soss brothers—"

"You're standing on your own grave," Fargo warned him, an edge of impatience creeping into his voice. "I don't care a frog's fat ass who made the damn thing. You were here when it rolled in. Give me the particulars."

Crazy Charlie gouged a finger into his nose again and Fargo, disgusted, averted his eyes. "Well, it was maybe ten days ago or so. She come in, all right, doors flapping. Nary a soul on her. The manifest listed no passengers, but Rudy Steele, the driver, and Joshua Robinson, the express messenger, were missing."

"So the Stanton brothers went looking for them?"

Crazy Charlie assumed a lecherous grin. "You seen their women, hanh? Gonna getcher package wrapped, hanh? I seen 'em naked. Laws! They—"

Fargo wagged the barrel of his Colt. "You're taking the long way around the barn, mooncalf. I asked about the brothers, not the gals."

"Yeah, they rode out. Didn't come back neither. Then a mail rider came by, said their dead bodies was back down the federal road a few miles. The horses was gone. Me and him fetched 'em and buried the bodies out back of the station."

"Killed by Indians or whites?"

"Full of bullets, not arrows."

Fargo nodded. "All right. What do you know about the strongbox?"

"Never seen that, neither. That Kreeger gang musta got it."

"They don't have it," Fargo said. "And neither do the Flatheads. That leaves you or the widows. Or both. Now which is it?"

"Why do they call 'em Flatheads?" Crazy Charlie wondered aloud. "Their heads ain't no flatter than yours or mine."

Fargo sighed and leathered his shooter. "Christ, I might's

15

well question a cross-eyed cow. Why the hell are you hanging around a place this dangerous? Overland has abandoned this route. Good chance you'll die of lead colic if you don't light a shuck out of here."

Crazy Charlie cut a little jig. "Leave? Mr. Fargo, I'm crazy, not stupid. Them three sisters is staying, ain't they? Now and again they let me see their tits."

Fargo narrowed his eyes in puzzlement. "Now why would they show you their tits?"

"To keep me on the place. I can hold and squeeze with a rifle, and several times now we've fought off raids by the Kreeger gang. And I've scared Injins off. They show the white feather when they meet a crazy paleface."

"You just got done saying," Fargo reminded him, "that you think the Kreeger gang laid hands on that strongbox. So why in hell would they be raiding this station?"

"Tarnation, Fargo, maybe *you're* a mite tetched. You seen them gals—ripe fruit waiting to be plucked. Or a word that rhymes with plucked. Dub Kreeger has set his sights on the youngest, Marlene. He's been thinking on that stuff until he's wound up to a fare-thee-well. He means to ride that filly and ride her hard."

For a crazy man Charlie suddenly made sense. Fargo had seen how a fetching woman could addle a man's think-piece, especially in the woman-starved West where men outnumbered females as much as two hundred to one. In a land where men were willing to marry the first thing off the stagecoach, teeth not required, any one of the Stanton sisters was an erotic jewel.

"All that shines," Fargo admitted as he swung open the barn door and whistled in the Ovaro. Dundee's sorrel followed the stallion. "But something ain't quite jake around here. Those women are playing it cagey and so are you. All three of those girls are mighty easy to look at, all right, and maybe the Kreeger gang really is sticking because the rut need is on them. But that's all the more reason the sisters should want to make tracks out of Robert's Station."

Crazy Charlie heaved a disconsolate sigh, then hummed the funeral march. "Poor little innocent goslings! Their beloved husbands lie fresh in the grave, and the iron bonds of matrimony—"

"Stick it where the sun doesn't shine," Fargo cut in. "I won't swallow your bunk. You got clean straw?"

"And hay. It's all up in the loft. Won't last much longer, though. I got the three team horses to board. Now yours makes two more."

"What happened to the fourth team horse?"

"The offside leader got wounded in the attack. I had to put him down. I don't know jackstraws about butchering anything bigger'n a rabbit, so the meat was wasted."

Fargo led each horse to a straw-lined stall. "What about the relay team that should've been here?"

"Indians turned 'em loose. Say, did you know that little Indian whelps suck at the dug until they're old enough to walk and follow the tit around? And a growed Indian has no hair on his pecker. Now—"

"Sew up your lips," Fargo ordered, "or I'll kill you for cause. You're s'pose to be crazy, not a runny mouth."

As if responding to Fargo's reminder, Crazy Charlie threw back his head and barked like a dog. Then he began capering about as he recited:

"Screwed your mama on a pile of rice,
Out come two babies shootin' dice,
One shot six, the other shot seven,
None a them motherhumpers goin' to heaven!"

Despite his disgust, Fargo chuckled. He averted his eyes, however, when Crazy Charlie again rammed a finger inside his nose.

"Boys," Dub Kreeger said, "I was afraid of this. Now we're in one world of hurt. I thought I recognized that lanky bastard earlier. Now I've seen the toothpick in his boot and that Henry, I know damn well who he is. We're gonna play hell getting that swag from those bitches now."

Dub's lean, hard face seemed carved out of bone. Fats Munro, Link Jeffries, and Willy Hanchon lay sprawled out beside him on a rock ledge overlooking Robert's Station. Dub handed the field glasses to Fats.

"He's hauling his tack inside the barn," Dub added. "I'll

bet my horse he means to stick around. Matter fact, I'd wager he's been hired by the army to find that strongbox. He's done a shitload of jobs for the army."

"Who is he?" Fats asked, busy peering through the glasses.

"You've heard tell of him. All of you have. Like I said he's done plenty of work for the army over the years, everything from scouting to running down deserters like us. His name is Skye Fargo."

Fats, who was actually skinny as a sapling but leather tough, let loose a piercing whistle. "Fargo, huh? I hear that son of a bitch is all grit and a yard wide. The Trailsman they call him. I hear he can track an ant across rocks and his gun hand is quicker than thought."

Willy Hanchon snorted. He was a furtive little rodent who never faced an opponent if he could shoot him in the back. He had tiny red ratlike eyes and constantly made nervous gestures. "What *I* hear about Fargo is that he's a pussy hound. He'll be more interested in getting under them bitches' petticoats than in the strongbox. Looks like he might bull that little blonde before you do, Dub."

"Skye Fargo can hum two songs at once," Dub assured him, ignoring his last remark. "He'll top the gals *and* get that money. Don't underrate him, boys. The road to hell is paved with the bones of men who took him lightly."

Link Jeffries, the fourth man in this gang of deserters, spat contemptuously. He was barrel-chested with muscular forearms like ninepins. He was a useful but dangerous dimwit who flew into rages only Dub could control.

"If Fargo's so rough," he said, "how's come he couldn't save Jasper Dundee today? Dub popped him over with one shot."

Dub smiled at the memory. "Yeah, that was some pumpkins, hey? Felt damn good, too. That son of a bitch Dundee once had me bucked and gagged just on account I stole some fruit from the mess hall. Now he can pull rank in hell."

"Sure, but it don't take away from Fargo," Fats reminded them. "Hell, it makes him even more dangerous. You killed his trail pard."

Dub nodded at this. "Fargo is hell on two sticks. We'll get that strongbox, all right, or I'll eat my shell belt. Matter fact, his arrival just might be providential for us."

"How you figure that?" Fats demanded.

"Good chance he'll do what we can't—get them gals out of the station and on the trail. With the gold."

"Sounds jim-dandy to me," Willy said. "I'm damn tired of sleeping rough, and we're damn near out of chewin's."

"But we'll still have to use wit and wile, boys, wit and wile. And meantime we got to hang on to our scalps—these red arabs around here are pissing blood since this road went through."

"Are you sure," Willy chimed in, "that the women really got that box?"

"Puzzle it out, chucklehead. We done for their husbands, so *they* ain't got it. We was about to grab it when the red sons attacked us, and that spooked the team horses toward the way station. The Injins only shot a few arrows into the coach then lit out after us. The coach is sitting at Robert's Station, and the women and that halfwit were the only ones there."

"Which means," Willy countered, "that the halfwit could have it. But the way them women been fighting us, I'm thinking they got it stashed somewhere."

Dub nodded. "Don't make no never mind. The halfwit, the bitches—they're all still there."

"And now," Fats said, "so is Skye goddamn Fargo."

Dub nodded. "True, and we ain't gonna rate him short. But I ain't never heard of a 'frontier legend' yet that didn't die some time."

"Besides," Fats said, "there's the savages. Fargo and Dundee were able to avoid them riding up, but getting back will be a whole nuther deal. They got them three sisters to save but only two saddle horses. Overland don't use combination horses broke to leather, so four of them horses is useless as tits on a boar hog. That means riding double. No way on God's green earth can they outrun Injun mustangs riding double."

Dub's carved-in-bone face creased in a smile. "You struck a lode there, chumley. And Fargo, he's a jobber—he ain't going no place without that gold. Remember, boys, the cat sits by the gopher hole. We'll just bide our time and watch for the main chance. Them pert skirts can fight, all right, but it's Fargo we have to kill first."

4

Fargo soon learned that the lovely Stanton widows had plenty of frontier savvy. Knowing an attack could come at any time, they kept their weapons placed at the three vulnerable sides of the station: the front and both side walls. Besides the Volcanic rifle—which held an impressive thirty shots in its huge magazine—and the double-ten express gun Marlene had held on him earlier, there were two Remington single-action revolvers and a Colt Navy.

"How you set for ammo?" Fargo asked when he returned from the barn.

"Only ten shells left for the scattergun," Darlene reported. "About a hundred shells for the Volcanic. We've got forty rounds for the Remingtons and about thirty for the Colt."

Fargo picked up one of the Remingtons and broke open the loading gate to inspect it. "Well, I stocked up before I left Fort Seeley. Plenty of loads for my Henry and my sidearm. We'll hold Jasper Dundee's carbine and firearm in reserve. That's plenty of firearms, but we're under siege here, and in a siege ammo tends to go fast. I'd give a purty to have more shells for that double ten. Damn useful weapon in a siege."

"Don't forget Crazy Charlie," Marlene put in, flashing her dimples at Fargo. "He's got him a bolt-action Prussian army rifle. And a whatchacallit—a bando, a bando—"

"A bandolier," Fargo supplied.

"Uh-huh, one a them just full of shells."

Fargo picked up the second Remington to inspect it. "It's a good rifle. I looked at it out in the barn. You say he can use it?"

"You wouldn't know he was crazy to see him in a gun battle," Darlene said. "I saw him blow a hole clear through an Indian's head."

"I thought his specialty was scaring them away?"

Sharlene laughed. She hadn't kept her eyes off Fargo since he came back inside. "Oh, it scared 'em, all right. They lit out like their butts was on fire."

Fargo scowled at the weapon, checking the trigger play. "You girls need to take a care with this shooter. It's got a worn sear."

Sharlene batted her eyes. "Is that bad?"

"Sure it's bad—dangerous. Makes the weapon hair trigger. It could discharge if you drop it."

Darlene had been watching her sister flirt. "That ain't the only thing around here that's hair trigger," she said, aiming a quelling stare at Sharlene. "Your Lemuel ain't even got grass growing over his grave yet and here you are giving bedroom eyes to Mr. Fargo."

"Mind your own bee's wax," Sharlene retorted. "I don't see you wearing no widow's weeds."

"That's on account we ain't got none," Marlene pitched in.

"That don't give you the right to act like whores," Darlene objected. "Mr. Fargo here has behaved like a gentleman."

"No bout adoubt it," Fargo declared, laying the Remington back down on the puncheon floor. "I'm a saint. Look, girls, this is no place to roost right now. You're trapped here, and the mouse that has but one hole is quickly taken."

Darlene gave him a lidded gaze. "You're in such an all-fired hurry to herd us out of here, but what about your precious gold? You said you can't leave without it."

"I figured you ladies would help me with that."

"Well, we won't," Darlene said flatly.

"Won't or can't?"

"Can't," Darlene said, smiling wickedly.

Fargo dropped it for the moment. "Since you got all these loopholes and no windows, I recommend you take turns watching for enemies. The Flatheads won't attack after sunset, so they're most dangerous by day. Kreeger and his graveyard rats are most likely to sneak in by night."

"That's how it's been," Darlene confirmed. "So far both groups have been easy to drive off."

Fargo nodded. "Most redskins don't like to attack a forted-up position. Buildings give them the fantods. As for

Kreeger's gang, they're cowards like most deserters. They want that gold, all right"—here Fargo glanced at Marlene—"and other treasures, too. But they don't want to die for it. That doesn't mean they aren't dangerous. And as I saw today, at least one of them is a by-God marksman. They'll keep working at it until they come up with a plan. Don't let your guard down."

"Yes, girls," Darlene told her sisters, "don't let your guard down."

Fargo saw another catfight about to erupt and quickly stepped outside to reconnoiter the area. He didn't trust any of these gals, especially Darlene. He got the distinct impression that her sisters' chastity was the least of her concerns. More like it, she was having second thoughts about letting him stay on because it placed that payroll money in jeopardy.

He stood in the shadow of the building and slowly swept the area with narrowed eyes. It was the middle of a crisp afternoon in the high country. A cloudless sky of bottomless blue left the surrounding mountain peaks starkly outlined. A red-tailed hawk circled high overhead, looking for prey. It was a craggy vista of talus slopes and basalt turrets—harsh, unforgiving country.

Henry rifle cradled in his left arm, Fargo began a slow circle of the station. While it had been a fool's mission to establish a stage line this high in the mountains, Fargo had to admit that Robert's Station was well situated for defense. Besides its thick walls there was a steep drop-off behind and exposed ground on the other three sides.

A drunken voice drifted to him from the barn:

"Down by the lake where nobody goes,
Stood a long-haired maiden without any clothes,
Along came Charlie swinging a chain,
Pulled open his fly and out it came.
Three months later all was well,
Six months later she began to swell,
Nine months later out it came:
A bow-legged soft brain swinging a chain."

Fargo shook his head but couldn't help grinning. He crossed to the barn and swung open the door. Crazy Charlie

22

lay in the filthy straw of his stall, swilling liquor from a crockery jug.

"Just maybe you are crazy," Fargo remarked. "Here you are, drunk as the lords of creation, and enemies all around you. You should be up in that loft keeping watch."

Crazy Charlie giggled. "Can't, long-shanks. I'll roll out the damn loft door and break my neck. Getting pickled can't be did carelessly."

Fargo cursed quietly and wrenched the jug from his hands, emptying it into the straw. Charlie watched him from baleful eyes. "What, you one a them temperance biddies?"

Fargo yanked him to his feet and backhanded him several times. "All of us are trapped between the sap and the bark. It's soon coming down to the nut-cuttin', mooncalf, and either you shape up or I'll kick your ass so hard you'll have to take off your hat to piss. Savvy that?"

Crazy Charlie nodded. "Savvy that."

"All right." Fargo let him go. "From now on you sleep up in the loft so you can see and hear what's going on. Tell me—those team horses. I noticed extra saddles and bridles in the tack room. Can you break three of those pulling horses to leather?"

"By the twin balls of Christ, Fargo! I'm a stock tender, not a peeler."

"So? You wrangle horses, don't you? No reason why you can't break 'em. They ain't mustangs, so you won't have to gentle them."

Crazy Charlie gave up with a shrug. "I'll see what I can do in that line, but I ain't a good man in a pinch."

"You can do it," Fargo said, not really believing it. "Now tell me something—where is that strongbox?"

"Why, where do all lost years go? Why ask a crazy son of a bitch like me?"

"Button, button, who's got the button?" Fargo muttered in disgust. "All right, get up in the loft and keep your eyes skinned."

Fargo found a pitchfork and went from stall to stall, poking the straw thoroughly. Next he carefully inspected the dirt floor of the barn for signs of recent burial. His search turned up a big goose egg.

A racket like a boar in rut reached him from the loft.

"Charlie!" he shouted. "Up and on the line!"

The snoring came to a stuttering halt. "Hunh? I ain't asleep, Fargo. It's just I got swollen adenoids."

"I don't know how, the way you always poke your finger into 'em. You best stay on the qui vive, crazy man, or I'll knock you into the middle of next week. You four been lucky so far, but the worm *will* turn, I guarandamntee it."

Fargo said this last as he climbed up into the loft with the pitchfork. Crazy Charlie saw it and cringed into a tight ball. "Christ, Fargo!" he screeched. "Don't poke me full of holes! It ain't right killing a crazy man. I—"

"Hush down, you fool. I ain't after you."

Fargo began a thorough search of the loft, poking and probing.

"You won't find nothing up here but a few dead rats," Charlie assured him.

"Yeah, and maybe one living rat," Fargo replied, aiming a speculative glance at the stock tender. "You would've been the first one to see that coach when it rolled in."

"I was dead drunk when it got here. The Stanton brothers were out in the yard."

Fargo found that plausible. "Did they take right off to find the driver and messenger?"

Charlie spread his hands in a helpless gesture. "Fargo, when I'm dead drunk I'm *dead* drunk."

Fargo muttered a curse as he continued searching. Now and then he crossed to the big loft door and gazed out at the surrounding terrain.

"Seems to me," he mused out loud, "the brothers would've at least taken the time to move that strongbox into the station."

Charlie assumed a deadpan face. "*If* it was on the coach."

"If it wasn't, those deserters wouldn't be attacking the station."

"You wouldn't say that, brother, if you ever seen the tits on them three sisters. That's a sight would make a dead man come."

Again Fargo had to agree with the disgusting fool. But he was convinced it had to be Dub Kreeger's gang who shot up that stagecoach, and if they had seized the money they would have dusted their hocks toward a city farther west.

"I have seen their tits," he finally answered. "All six of them and I've never seen any finer. But those tits ain't nothing to the matter. I got a notion either you or those gals have that money. Hell, maybe you're all in cahoots. You—"

"So you seen 'em too?" Crazy Charlie cut in eagerly. "So have I! They don't let me touch 'em, but a strapping young buck like you might get a taste. Moses on the mountain!"

Charlie threw back his head and howled like a wolf.

"Like I started to say," Fargo said sarcastically, "you could all be in cahoots. But that money is federal property and I was hired to find it. I'm not looking to jug anybody, and if you should decide to discover that strongbox, no harm done. If a U.S. marshal comes into this deal, it's a ball and chain for certain. And with the driver and shotgun messenger likely murdered into the deal, you just might be jerked to Jesus."

Charlie appeared to be solemnly listening. The moment Fargo fell silent, however, his moon face broke into a lecherous grin. "They all got magnificent tits, Fargo, but I like Marlene's the best. You notice how her nipples is pink and pointy? *Them's* good fixin's."

Fargo cursed and headed down out of the loft.

While there was still enough light, Fargo spent the next hour searching the area around the station on foot, not willing to risk exposing the Ovaro to dry-gulchers. He started close to the station and moved out in expanding circles. Several times he felt the back of his neck tingle and knew he was being watched. It was no comfort to recall the accurate shot that sent Captain Jasper Dundee across the River Jordan.

The mountain terrain was ruggedly beautiful but also difficult to search. The rocky slopes were covered with flat chunks of metamorphic rock, any one of which could conceal a small strongbox in a shallow hole. There were also numerous caves, and Fargo had to cautiously sniff before entering. Surprising a grizzly could be his last act on earth, especially since only a big-bore Sharps or Hawken buffalo gun could drop one.

25

The sun sank lower and Fargo started back toward Robert's Station, his senses alert but his mind constantly working. He knew he would need to do more searching of the area, but he reminded himself that the strongbox might be hidden at the station itself. He had noticed during his first circling of the building that a short, covered dogtrot behind the station led to three cubbyhole rooms. He had seen these plenty along stagecoach lines. They were usually equipped with cots of leather webbing and supplied as a courtesy to female passengers so they could nap during long layovers or during rough weather.

Maybe, Fargo thought, instead of sleeping in the barn with that crazy nose-picker who snored loud enough to wake snakes, he'd take turns with those three rooms. Even if nothing hidden turned up it put him closer to the station during attacks. Not to mention three pretty, shapely widows who didn't seem all that broken up with grief.

He grinned at the thought, but a moment later the grin was wiped away by the sharp, distinctive crack of a cavalry carbine.

5

Fargo's battle-trained ear told him immediately that the shot wasn't meant for him. It came from downslope, near the federal road, and was almost surely an attack on the way station. The Spencer carbine meant Dub Kreeger and his cutthroats—most likely they had been watching him from a distance, and once he was far enough away they launched this strike.

It was a dangerous task, running on this rocky talus slope, but Fargo moved down the mountain in long, springing bounds, holding his Henry at a high port. He focused down to the ground immediately in front of him and sought out landing places where his foot wouldn't slip. One tumble on this steep slope and with momentum behind him could spell disaster. Some of these shards of shale and flint were like knife blades, and he had seen men shredded to death before they finally stopped.

More carbines opened up, their hard crack echoing off the rock faces and sounding like an army. But the defenders had opened up, too. He could hear the Volcanic's popping sound, smaller caliber than the .56 carbines. And Crazy Charlie must have shaken off his drunken stupor—the impressive wallop of his bolt-action Prussian rifle reverberated up the slope.

A stray round struck sparks in the flint just ahead of him and Fargo flinched, momentarily losing his concentration. That moment turned into near disaster. Fargo's right foot slid off the flat rock he had aimed for, skidding into loose dirt and gravel.

He was moving fast and his right leg shot out from under him, sending him into a forward tumble that could have lasted for a hundred bruising yards. But he immediately brought his Henry down as a sort of cane, correcting the tumble in the nick of time. He reached the bottom of the slope and spotted the graded road and the besieged station just beyond it.

"There's Fargo!" a gravelly voice shouted from hawthorn thickets on Fargo's left. "Put at him, boys!"

Suddenly the air around Fargo's exposed position was blurry with lead, some of the bullets snapping past his ears so close he felt the wind-rip. He had little choice but to take up a prone position and count on the famous Henry, "the gun you load on Sunday and fire all week." Repeatedly the stock slapped his cheek as Fargo levered and fired, levered and fired, shredding hawthorn leaves as he peppered the thickets with lead.

The intimidating Henry did its job and did it well. First all firing stopped from the thickets, then Fargo heard horses escaping in a drumbeat of galloping hooves. He waited in place in case it was a feint and the gang was doubling back. But the sound of escape gradually died out.

"Good work, Mr. Fargo!" Darlene's voice called from inside the station. She could see him through the loopholes in the front wall. "I don't think any of 'em was hit, but they sure ran like a river when the snow melts. That rifle of yours is death to the devil."

Fargo started across toward the station. "This is why you ladies need to pack up and let me guide you down to Fort Seeley. This day alone I've busted twenty-six caps. Do the ciphering—these little harassing raids use up ammo fast. Kreeger and his bunch know that, and they know there's no resupply for us."

Marlene opened the door for him, staring at his powder-blackened face.

"Well, they shoot off ammo, too," Darlene argued. "And they got no resupply either."

Fargo shot a quick, appreciative glance at all three women. Sharlene flashed him a come-hither smile that Fargo could feel in his hip pocket.

"That's true," he answered Darlene, "but they don't need resupply—not of ammo anyhow. When they busted out of the hoosegow they took over a thousand rounds with them."

"Well, even if that's so, we ain't leaving yet," she said stubbornly. "And you ain't law duly sworn. Only a badge-toter can order us out of here."

Fargo loosed a long, weary sigh. "I told you I don't force women to do anything."

Darlene narrowed her eyes. "Like hob! Watching you out there, routing them four mean killers, didn't give me no impression that you're a reasonable man. You're use to being the cock of the dung heap."

"I'd hardly call you ladies a dung heap. Besides, *why* won't you leave? And don't hand me that malarkey about your husbands—it won't make them rest easier if you three get yourselves killed."

"We'll go when we're good and ready," Darlene said flatly.

"Time is a bird, lady, and the bird is on the wing. If Kreeger's bunch don't prevail, Flathead Indians will. The featherheads have backed off because of those new graves, but eventually they'll paint for battle and burn this place to the ground with us in it."

"If you're such a scaredy-cat," Darlene taunted him, "might be you best leave."

"He ain't no scaredy-cat," Marlene interjected, "and I don't want him to leave."

"Me neither," Sharlene chimed in, running the tip of her tongue over her upper lip for Fargo's benefit. "Crazy Charlie has spine in a fight, but Mr. Fargo ain't no halfwit."

As if this were his cue, Charlie's whiny voice sounded outside. "Ladies? I fought like a tiger. I'm here to collect my pay."

"Shit!" Darlene said. "That crazy old coot. Well, a deal's a deal, I reckon. Best let him in, Marlene."

"You pay him for every skirmish?" Fargo said, astounded.

"You might say that," Darlene replied. "He won't fight if we don't."

Fargo resolved to remedy that blackmail. Marlene swung open the heavy door and Charlie scampered inside.

"Ladies," he said, leering at them.

"All right, I did it last time," Darlene said. "Whose turn is it?"

"Mine," Sharlene spoke up quickly, slanting a flirtatious glance toward Fargo.

"I'm waiting," Charlie said, his moon face shiny with expectation.

"Get that finger outta your damn nose," Darlene snapped, "or no pay."

Fargo, completely baffled by now, waited for Sharlene to fetch some money. Instead, the raven-haired beauty unlooped the buttons of her bodice and opened her dress, baring a magnificent set of hard, high-riding breasts.

Crazy Charlie moaned as he stared, eyes popping. Fargo, too, was staring—and realizing he had no intention of interfering with Charlie's blackmail.

Charlie began capering about the room, still staring. "Yum-yum, eat 'em up! Just one little touch, Sharlene?"

Sharlene was too busy seeing how Fargo enjoyed the view to listen to Charlie.

"If you ever touch any of us," Darlene replied, "I'll smack you sick and silly. You smell like rotten tripes. Don't you never take a bath?"

"Why, is there one missing?"

Darlene gave an exasperated sigh. "All right, that's enough. Sharlene, close your dress. Charlie, get back to the barn."

"Can't move right now. I gotta rock-hard peck—"

"Get out!" Darlene ordered, crossing toward him. Charlie howled as he scuttled out the door.

Fargo shook his head in disbelief. "Well, that was pleasant enough. But I've gone wide upon the world, been to New Orleans and Manhattan and even Mexico City. I've seen two-headed cows and streams that flow uphill and men who sleep on beds of nails and walk on hot coals. But I've never seen the like of this."

"We got no choice," Marlene said. "The man is pure-dee crazy and thinks of nothing but titties. It's the only way we can get him to fight."

Fargo grinned. "Crazy? Like hell he is. What he's getting from you lasses is better than gold."

Even stern Darlene smiled at this compliment. "Mr. Fargo, no offense, but you're a mite whiffy yourself. There's a washtub out back, and a woodstove for heating water. We've got soap and towels, too."

"I like that idea," Fargo agreed. "I've been on the trail a while."

"I'll help you," Sharlene volunteered.

"Nix on that," Darlene snapped. "Both you girls just stay in the house. Mr. Fargo knows his own geography well enough to scrub it."

"The back is hard to scrub," Fargo said hopefully.

"Do your best," Darlene replied.

"Yeah," Fargo said without enthusiasm, still thinking of Sharlene's creamy, plum-tipped mounds.

The iron washtub sat out back in the small patch of ankle-high grass that suddenly ended in a steep drop-off. Fargo eyed the three new crosses and suddenly wondered: did those three cunning sisters perhaps kill their own husbands to seize that payroll money? Why else would such beauties be flashing their bare tits to a disgusting halfwit like Crazy Charlie? After all, he was the only other witness.

But then Fargo recalled the mail rider who had found the bodies well down the road. His story was part of an official report to Overland. And clearly these three sisters didn't shoot that coach full of arrows.

They likely had that money, all right, Fargo told himself as he dragged the tub under the dogtrot for protection. And they were dangerous—not murderers, he hoped, but dangerous to anyone who tried to take that gold from them. And here he was, trying to come between the dogs and their meat.

As if they weren't enough, there were four more dogs after that meat—Dub Kreeger and his minions. With Jasper Dundee gone under, Fargo knew he was on a hard trail bound straight for hell.

The old Franklin stove sat just beyond the dogtrot, stove-lengths of wood stacked all around it. Fargo heated buckets of water from a rainwater cistern until the tub was half-full, topping it with a bucket of cold water. He found a twisted knot of lye soap on a wooden shelf and peeled out of his buckskins, making sure to leave his Henry propped up close by and leaving his gun belt on the ground near the tub.

Hissing sharply at the heat he eased himself into the water, which he had not cooled enough. When it finally cooled tolerably he felt himself relaxing. He and Jasper had slept very little on the trail, and now Fargo's eyes felt weighted with coins.

"Mr. Fargo?"

Darlene's voice behind him made Fargo flinch. "Ma'am?"

"You forgot to grab you a towel. I'll put it here on top of your clothes."

"'Preciate it."

"Mr. Fargo, please don't get the impression that I'm ungrateful to you. If I seem suspicious-like it's only on account I got my sisters to protect."

Fargo sudsed his hair. "Do I seem dangerous to you?"

"Well, not dangerous like a criminal, no. But a man as strong and handsome as you *is* dangerous. Marlene and Sharlene are very vulnerable right now."

It cost Fargo an effort not to laugh outright. Darlene had them showing their tits to Crazy Charlie, and she had the gall to call them "vulnerable"?

"Could be you've also noticed," she added, "that they're very pretty."

"Uh-huh. And so are you."

"Yes, but I'm stronger than they are."

Fargo ducked his head to rinse it. "Yeah, I've noticed that. The ringleader usually is the strongest."

"The . . . what?"

"You know, the head hound, the topkick, the honcho. The one who cooked up the plan to steal that gold."

There was a long, awkward pause while Fargo washed the mat of curlicues on his chest.

Her voice had lost some of its charm when she finally replied. "Is that a fact or just a slander against me?"

"Lady, that's what they call a distinction without a difference. You won't find a circuit judge within three hundred miles of this spot, so bottle the 'slander' charge."

"Mr. Fargo, I understand you've spent your entire life on the frontier."

"Most of it, but I'm town-broke too."

"Well, we're in the Nebraska Territory, not a civilized state. Can you recall any time, in any territory, where a woman has ever been charged with a crime and taken to law for it?"

The menacing sound of a hammer being thumb-cocked made Fargo revolve slowly around to confront her. The muzzle of a Remington was pointed straight at his head.

"I take your point," Fargo conceded.

"I could blow your brains right out for what you just accused me of. And there ain't a man anywhere would challenge my right to do it."

"Just curious," Fargo said. "Is that the hair-trigger gun I was looking at earlier?"

Darlene flashed teeth like a double string of pearls. "It is. Maybe you'd like to swallow back your words before my finger twitches?"

Fargo sat out his next heartbeat. "Consider them swallowed."

"Good." Darlene swung the wheel out and gave Fargo a good look—all the cylinders were empty. "I just wanted to take you to school—I hope you learned your lesson."

She whirled around and went back into the station. Fargo did a slow burn. You could beat the truth out of a man, but women didn't play fair. Nonetheless, he was determined to recover that strongbox and return it to the U.S. Army. Once he hired on for a job he finished the damn thing, and no amount of feminine wiles or luscious tits were going to stop him.

He hoped.

Fargo finished his bath, dressed, and hauled the tub outside to empty it. Suddenly it occurred to him that his pockets literally felt lighter. He fished a hand into his right pocket, where he kept a chamois pouch filled with his money. The pocket was empty—the pouch and forty dollars in gold and silver were gone.

"I'll be hog-tied and earmarked," he muttered. "That high-toned slut cleaned me out."

That's why she gave him that little lecture about what happens to men who accuse women out west. If he went in there huffing and puffing about it now, she'd put an air shaft through him. And if he dared to defend himself, the law would have his guts for garters. Even the hardest outlaws tried to avoid killing women out west.

Fargo buckled on his gun belt. He was stuck in an unusual situation with three women who were shiftier than a creased buck. But in the end these were just three more fillies, and Fargo had never met a horse he couldn't ride.

6

Fargo, not once mentioning his stolen money pouch, talked to all three women and Crazy Charlie. Everyone agreed to divide the night up into five guard stints, Fargo taking the last from four a.m. until sunrise.

"You ladies have any objection," Fargo remarked just past sundown, "if I bed down in one of the three rooms out back? Crazy Charlie snores great guns. Besides, I don't want to get cut off from the station if a lead bath commences."

The three women were playing stud poker at one of the trestle tables. They exchanged a quick glance at Fargo's suggestion.

"If that's your plan to . . . visit one of us in the night," Darlene replied, slapping down a discard, "it won't work. The three of us all sleep in that bedroom off the kitchen."

Marlene tittered. "I don't think even a strapping buck like you, Mr. Fargo, would be up to . . . visiting all three of us."

"Not at one time," Fargo confessed with regret. "That would be an embarrassment of riches."

"Ain't *he* the charming saddle bum?" Darlene said, her tone sarcastic. "Sure, you can have one of the rooms, Mr. Fargo. I'm not sure we can trust you, but we all sleep with our weapons, and all three of us can shoot."

"Not sure you can trust *me*?" Fargo shot back, glancing at the gold cartwheels and silver dollars piled in front of Darlene. "That stake in front of you, darling, looks awful familiar. Just about forty dollars, I'd say."

Darlene's Remington lay on the table near her right hand. She curled her fingers around the walnut grip and looked at him asquint. "Why, Mr. Fargo, if you got a point, feel free to make it."

You thieving bitch, Fargo thought. But he forced a smile. "Nah, just an idle remark."

"How are your pasteboard skills?" Darlene added. "We could use a fourth hand."

Fargo perked up. His pasteboard skills were formidable indeed, and this might be a chance to win that purloined money back.

"Deal me in, ladies," he said, adding pointedly, "but I'm a might short on cash. I seem to have mislaid my money pouch."

"That's a shame," Darlene remarked with false unction, and Fargo had to restrain himself from slapping the beautiful bitch.

While Darlene dealt, Marlene said, "If you sleep up here, Mr. Fargo, that'll leave Crazy Charlie alone in the barn."

"According to him, he's been alone in the barn anyway. Besides, that's the most easily defended building, what with that big loft door. Even if somebody gets inside, he's got a dozen good places to hole up. Whether it's Kreeger's gang or Flathead Indians, this building will be the main target. Which is why I wish you ladies would reconsider the idea of pulling out."

"All in good time," Darlene said, mulling her cards. "Besides, how would we ride down to the flats? You came in with only two horses. The rest are team horses—unless you plan on hitching them to that Overland coach?"

Fargo sorted his cards and anted up. "That would be a fool's errand. A coach would have to take the new federal road—we'd be a bug on a tabletop. There's a few old mountain-man traces we can ride down that are better protected. I've got Charlie working on saddle-breaking the three pulling horses."

All three sisters broke into laughter at this announcement. "Charlie and 'working' are two words that don't fit together," Marlene said. "You'll see an oyster walk upstairs before that disgusting lout ever does a lick of work."

Fargo scowled at his worthless hand—no pairs and nothing

higher than the six of clubs. "He'll get it done. There's ways to motivate a man. Earlier I tossed his liquor."

As if timed to prove Fargo had much to learn, a drunken verse reached them from the barn:

"Lulu had a chicken,
Lulu had a duck,
Put 'em on the table
To see if they would
Bang, bang Lulu,
Bang 'er every day,
Who's gonna bang poor Lulu
When I get old and gray?"

"He's s'pose to be on sentry duty," Fargo said.

Darlene sent Fargo a smarmy grin. "Crazy Charlie has cheap wagon-yard liquor stashed all over that barn. You'll have to burn it down to get every jug. Discards, Mr. Fargo?"

"Three," Fargo said from a deadpan, already realizing he had stepped in quicksand. Sure enough, his three new cards left him without a pair and the nine of hearts as high card. Out of spite he decided to bluff. A minute later every bung-town copper he had left sat in front of Darlene.

"That knife in your boot is a fine piece of work," she suggested. "Slap it on the table and I'll call it three dollars credit."

"His hat is fine work," Marlene chimed in, "but too many bullet holes. Maybe we could go a dollar on it."

Fargo stood up, looking like a man who was waking up in the middle of the wrong week. "Ladies, I best quit before I'm naked. I've been cleaned out fast before, but never in the first hand."

Darlene's emerald green eyes bored into him. "Is that another accusation, Mr. Fargo?"

"No, just a notice of surrender."

"Play a few more hands," Sharlene urged, flashing him an up-and-under smile. "Won't trouble me one bit to see you naked."

"Don't encourage him," Darlene snapped. "Skye Fargo chases more tail than a dizzy dog."

"And generally catches what he chases," Fargo added

spitefully. He prided himself on his mastery over pretty women, but these diabolical sisters had robbed his pockets and cheated him at cards, all on the first night. How soon before they scalped him and ate his horse?

"Just maybe," Darlene told him, "you been chasing the two-bit merchandise too long. Now you've run smack-dab into the top-shelf goods, and just maybe it's out of your price range, handsome drifter."

She paused long enough to let that acid sizzle into him, then added with cloying sweetness, "Good night, Mr. Fargo. And sweet dreams. That's all you're going to enjoy around here."

Fargo went out to the barn and was surprised to discover that Crazy Charlie, though sipping from a jug, wasn't yet carrying a brick in his hat.

"Didja get to play with any titties?" he greeted Fargo eagerly.

"Old son, all I got was that free show Sharlene gave you. Matter fact, I'm lucky Darlene didn't turn me into a sieve. Say, is that all you think about are titties?"

"Think, dream, scheme. Titties is the only part of a woman I care about. A pretty face, a well-turned ankle, even that hairy cave betwixt their legs—I wouldn't give a plugged peso for any of it. Give me tits."

Fargo shook his head in the sterling shaft of moonlight streaming into the loft. "Sounds like maybe you were shorted on milk when you were just a pup on the rug. Been quiet so far?"

"I seen a grizzly out front of the station about a half hour ago. But it took off when I fired up a lamp."

"Up this high in the mountains there'll be plenty," Fargo remarked. "Especially with hibernation over. Don't forget they're winter-starved and plenty dangerous."

"They won't eat a crazy man," Charlie boasted. "Gives 'em dyspepsia."

Fargo eyed him in the moon wash. "You know where that money is, don't you?"

Charlie shifted on his bale of hay. "To chew it fine, I'm crazy, not stupid. If I had twenty-eight thousand dollars in

37

gold, I wouldn't be up here drinking panther piss. A man could walk out of here and back to civilization in four days."

"I didn't say it was yours to take and spend. I think those sisters have it and they've gone snooks with you if you sew up your lips about it. Or they *say* they'll go snooks because you're a good hand with that rifle of yours and they want protection until they can skedaddle from here. Truth to tell, when they can get clear they'll paper these barn walls with your brains."

Crazy Charlie screeched with laughter. "Here's the man, all tattered and torn, who kissed the maiden all forlorn."

"It's clear as a blood spoor in new snow," Fargo persisted, ignoring the outburst. "That's why they bare their tits practically on demand. They're keeping you tethered to this place until they don't need you anymore. Charlie, don't let some tempting titties and the promise of gold you'll never see lure you into an unnamed grave. Throw in with me and I'll see that you get the ten percent recovery fee. That's damn near three thousand dollars, stout lad—a soldier would have to serve fifteen years to make that much."

"Forty miles a day on beans and hay in the regular army, *oh!*"

Fargo resisted the urge to yank the soft-brain to his feet and smack some sense into him. He had been handed some queer jobs in his day, but between those alluring pit vipers in the house and this nose-picking halfwit in the barn, Fargo was beginning to wonder if the teeming cities back east were as crazy as he remembered.

"Never mind the beans and hay," he said mildly. "Did you get going on saddle-breaking those horses?"

"I commenced on the big roan with the blazed forehead. I almost got him taking a bridle."

"Good man. Keep working on 'em. We need all three so nobody rides double. And go gradual on that cheer water. I want you at least half-ass sober if trouble comes. This is no time for anybody to fall asleep at the switch."

"Them that drink whiskey will think whiskey, right?"

Fargo started for the ladder. "Right."

"Well, then, them that drink water will think water!" Crazy Charlie threw after him triumphantly.

"Jesus Katy Christ," Fargo muttered as he started down the ladder. "What in the *hell* am I doing here?"

7

Fargo borrowed a coal-oil lamp from a crosstree in the stock barn and inspected the three small rooms behind the station house. All three contained only a ladder-back chair, a lantern on a keg, and a sturdy cot of leather webbing. He selected the middle room, pulled in the latchstring, and propped his Henry against a wall. He hung his gun belt from the back of the chair and removed only his boots, placing his Arkansas toothpick handy on the floor near the bed.

Despite his exhaustion Fargo paced the tiny room for several minutes, smoking a thin black Mexican cigar and fuming over the theft of his money. If a man had skinned him like that, the brazen son of a bitch would be feeding worms by now. But Darlene had demurely taunted him with her knowing smile—and then cleaned him out by cheating at poker! That was another frontier offense that would be resolved by the undertaker if the haughty vixen was a man.

Eventually, however, the Trailsman's sense of irony and humor prevailed, and his lips eased apart in a smile. Hell, he required little money anyway, and he couldn't help admiring a woman who could bamboozle him like that. He took it as a warning, however, to keep a wary eye out for these three treacherous beauties—especially Darlene.

Fargo stretched out on the cot, still grinning, and almost immediately tumbled down a long tunnel into a dreamless sleep. He had no idea how long he'd been out when a persistent scratching at the door woke him with a start. He wrapped his right hand around the handle of his long knife.

"Mr. Fargo?" came a whispered voice. "Are you awake?"

"I am now. Who is it?"

"It's me—Sharlene? Can I come in? Darlene's on guard and I don't want her to catch me."

Fargo scratched a lucifer to life and lifted the chimney of the lamp, firing up the wick. Then he traded the knife for his Colt and opened the door.

Sharlene, wearing only a thin anchor-print dress, spurted inside and closed the door. She stared at the six-gun. "I reckon you ain't too happy to see me."

"You reckon wrong, lass. I'm just a cautious man."

Her pretty face was burnished with gold by the lamplight. The wild tumble of thick black hair framed her face and made her look both angelic and wanton.

"I reckon you wonder why I'm here," she said, flashing him a coy smile.

"That's not the *first* thing on my mind," he admitted.

Her emerald-sheening eyes told him that was the right answer. "Mr. Fargo, could I get your opinion on something?"

"If you think it's worth anything, sure."

"Oh, it is. You must be an expert on such matters. See, Darlene and Marlene both think my nipples are too big. Do you?"

As casually as if she were unwrapping groceries, she unlooped the buttons of her garment, letting the anchor-print dress fall off her shoulders. Fargo had to adjust his position as a rush of hot blood uncoiled his man gland.

"Are they too big?" she fretted.

Fargo's mouth was suddenly only scant inches away from the succulent mounds of two of the finest tits he'd ever gazed upon—hefty, firm, ivory white, and capped by strawberry-colored nipples that tapered to firm points. All at once he understood Charlie's obsession. He didn't buy her big-eyed act for one moment, but this was one trail he intended to ride to the end.

"See?" she said in a plaintive voice. "Darlene's the oldest and she says my nipples cover too much of my titties. You're a man—do *you* think so?"

"The way they are right now, no. They're perfect, muffin. But the real test comes when they're . . . excited."

Sharlene fluttered her curving lashes, still playing the ingénue. "You mean . . . like how they get when it's cold?"

Fargo fought to keep a straight face. "Uh-huh. Or better yet—when they're sucked on."

"But I can't reach my mouth down there."

"Well, then, allow me." Fargo bent forward and took one of those chewy gumdrops into his mouth. It stiffened immediately, probing deeper into his mouth. He swirled his tongue around it rapidly. Darlene gasped and shuddered, gripping his shoulders to support herself.

"Mr. Fargo, my stars alive! It's easy to see you've done this before."

Fargo pulled back and studied his handiwork. The nipple was so hard it looked like the tip of a Mexican lance.

"Definitely not too big," he assured her. "Matter fact, that just might be the most perfect nipple I've ever seen."

In truth Fargo had pleasured so many it was impossible to remember them all, but it seemed like the thing to say. His tone was that of an objective man judging prize roses. But she hardly seemed to hear him. Her breathing was rapid and ragged, and she moved one hand from his muscle-corded shoulder to twine her fingers in his thick, unruly thatch of hair.

"Well?" she asked him in a husky voice, glancing at the cot.

"Well what, Sharlene?"

Her nostrils flared. "Well *what*? You got my naughty parts tingling, that's what! You think you can just toss a match into the kerosene and then go to sleep?"

Fargo's strong white teeth flashed in a grin. "Nope. You're gonna take care of this pants-buster you gave me. But I suspect your sisters sent you in here to distract me, maybe so they can shoot me or conk me on the cabeza and search my saddlebags."

"Skye! How can you—"

"Bottle it," he said without anger. "You and me are gonna do the mazy waltz, all right. But you had better call off the dogs because I sure would hate to shoot them while I'm trimming their sister."

Sharlene shimmied out of her dress and sat naked on the cot. "That *was* the plan," she admitted shamelessly. "Not to shoot you, only to bash you on the bean. Darlene wants to see your orders from the fort. But I never planned to go along—check the door. I pulled the latchstring in so she can't open it."

"I appreciate that, but Darlene is a willful woman. It might push her to shoot me."

"Nuh-unh. None of us are too keen to waste a man like you. We're lots safer now, and of course, you're mighty pleasing to look on. And look—"

She indicated the tiny room with a wave of one slim white hand. "No windows. She can't shoot at you even if she wants to. You still suspicious?"

Fargo raked his eyes over the naked beauty. "I am, but this is the point where a man has to throw caution to the winds."

He grabbed his gun belt off the chair and set it on the floor next to the lamp. "Now let's cut the palaver and get thrashing."

He untied his buckskins and let them drop. Darlene did a double take, then a triple take, when she caught sight of his angry, swollen manhood, so engorged with excited blood that it leaped with each heartbeat like a hound at feeding time.

"I ain't seen many of those," she assured him in a reverent tone, "but if that thing was any bigger you'd need a third shoe."

She stretched out on the leather webbing, locking her hands behind her head. Fargo felt his pulse boost from a lope to a gallop. In the flattering light of the lantern she looked like a coquette in a French masterpiece: a flowing mane of jet-black hair, creamy, flawless skin like lotion, high, firm breasts, and a generous "V" of mons hair. Her hips flared out like an hourglass.

Suddenly the door rattled. Darlene's voice: "Sharlene! What in tarnal blazes are you doing in there?"

"You were a married woman," she replied, holding her succulent tits as if in offering to Fargo. "Figure it out."

"You stupid bitch! You was just suppose to—"

Darlene caught herself in the nick of time. Fargo grinned as he reached down and separated Sharlene's supple thighs. She opened them even wider, inviting him, and Fargo wriggled into the saddle. The glistening pink canyons and folds of her sex yawned wide for him. He bent his shaft until the hard purple dome eased into her portal, caressing her sensitive pearly nubbin.

"Oh, Moses on the mountain!" she cried out as she slid her hands under his shirt. "*Give* it to me, Skye!"

"*I'll* give it to you, you damn bitch in heat," Darlene muttered on the other side of the door.

Fargo flexed his ass, sinking his length into Sharlene and parting the elastic walls of her love tunnel. It felt like red ants were biting into him as she dug her fingernails into his back. Hot, tight pleasure poured over his shaft and Sharlene wrapped her legs tight around him as he pounded harder and faster.

"Do me *harder*!" she commanded after several shivering climaxes stoked her lust. "Hard and fast!"

Fargo was happy to oblige. He hadn't made the two-backed beast with a woman in several weeks. He took it from a gallop to a breakneck run, plumbing her depths in furious plunges that made her emit sharp little cries of pleasure.

"Sharlene!" her sister's worried voice called from without. "You all right?"

Sharlene ignored her, pretty face twisted in indescribable pleasure as the ultimate climax racked her in shuddering spasms. Fargo pushed himself up on his fists and made his conclusive thrusts, exploding inside her and collapsing on her in a weak daze, gasping for breath.

For several minutes the two of them lay in a stupor, only slowly surfacing to awareness. Then Darlene's miffed voice again assaulted their ears. "Sharlene, get your ass out here!"

"Why?" Sharlene's lazy voice replied. "Mr. Fargo's been gettin' *his* in here!"

Fargo snorted, Darlene fumed, and Sharlene's exploring hand discovered that the Trailsman was ready to saddle up again.

False dawn, the time when the night sky began to lighten just before sunrise, found Dub Kreeger and his fellow deserters ensconced among boulders only about one hundred yards above Robert's Station. Their horses were hobbled behind a deadfall in back of them.

"Won't be long now, boys," Kreeger said, staring into the grainy light. "Fargo has to come out sooner or later and cross to that barn. He rates that Ovaro of his aces high, and he won't trust the halfwit to tend to him proper. We'll have four carbines and one clear chance to knock him out from under his hat."

"Well he best hold off a mite," Fats Munro fretted. "Fargo ain't the kind to burn daylight in bed—if he don't wait till sunrise we won't have a good bead on him."

"From what I hear of Fargo," Willy Hanchon chimed in, "he's been poking one of those gals all night. He won't be bright-eyed and bushy-tailed. Hell, Dub, might be he's been topping that little blonde you're all het up about."

Kreeger had indeed been stewing over that possibility. "Right now that's small potatoes," he snapped. "We'll sup full of poon after we kill Fargo. I got me a gut hunch them tricky little bitches got that gold hid somewhere. You might say them three's the keys to the mint. But so long as Fargo is above the ground, we ain't gonna find out where it's stashed."

Link Jeffries had been quietly listening to all this. "You figure it's hid in the station, Dub?" he asked.

"If it is, Fargo will find it. That canny bastard could find a splinter in an elephant's ass. So we best hope it *ain't* in the station—or the stock barn. Only them three bitches know. And maybe Crazy Charlie."

"So we best kill Fargo pronto," Fats echoed his boss. "That's my credo."

Dub nodded, shivering in the early morning chill. "Right as rain. We missed the main chance, chums, when we failed to kill him yesterday on the trail. Now we—hey! Snap into it, boys! I see a light moving through the loopholes. Somebody's stirring. If Fargo holds off another fifteen minutes, we'll have enough light to shoot him to doll stuffings."

8

Fargo had deliberately assigned himself the last stint of guard duty so he could make an initial search of the main room of the station house while the sisters slept.

He began with a close, minute search of the puncheon floorboards. These were perhaps a foot wide with half-inch gaps between them. It was tedious work, but he ran the long blade of his Arkansas toothpick through every crack. However, he felt nothing but hard-packed dirt.

While he worked, picking up splinters in his knees, he cast wary glances toward the door of the widows' bedroom. After being stymied last night in her plan to knock him out, Darlene might resort to something more drastic. Fargo tried to never shoot a woman, but if one tried to plug him he was damned if he would sit still for it.

When he finally finished he glanced overhead. Nothing but a few narrow crossbeams.

"Looking for something, Mr. Fargo?"

Darlene's sudden voice made Fargo flinch. She stood in the middle of the big main room, wearing nothing but a thin linen wrapper.

"That should be no big surprise," he told her calmly. "You know what I was sent here for."

"Yes. You were sent here for me and my sisters. So far you 'got' Sharlene."

Fargo shrugged one shoulder. "She stopped by for a visit last night, sure."

Darlene threw back her head and laughed. "Visit? That's high and deep, buckskins! You had her barking like a dog."

"What of it? She's free, white, and twenty-one."

"All true. And her husband's barely cold in the grave."

45

"It's always the lady's choice with me. She knocked on my door."

"Oh, you just drip virtue," Darlene snapped. "You'd screw a snake if somebody would hold its mouth open."

Fargo chuckled. "Don't come preaching to me, lady. You're just steamed because your little plan to coldcock me and search my saddlebags came a cropper."

"Wrong again, crop beard. While you were out here stabbing the dirt, I searched your bags thoroughly."

"Find what you needed?"

The smug smile melted from her face. "You know I didn't. I found beef jerky, some disgusting dried fruit, field glasses, bandage cloth, strips of rawhide, some cigars that smell like an outhouse—but no orders."

"That's because there aren't any—not cut on paper, anyhow. But of course you want to know what the army has to say about the gold shipment, eh?"

"It's only natural," she said demurely. "Doesn't everyone around here want to know about it? You're always harping on it."

"Speaking for myself, I'd sure like to know where it is."

"So you can *return* it, right?"

Fargo nodded. "What else? That's what I was hired to do."

Darlene narrowed her wing-shaped eyes. "Ah, the man of virtue again. The same callous lecher who takes advantage of a grieving widow has no plans at all for stealing that gold. Nor orders to prove he was sent for it."

"You've already hatched that plan to steal it. And roped your sisters into it."

"Says you. If I did know where it was, I wouldn't tell you."

Fargo snorted. "Lady, if God Himself climbed this mountain to take charge of that gold you wouldn't surrender it. But just think about it: the longer you delay, waiting for the right time to hightail it with that color, the more danger you and your sisters face. You been lucky so far, but luck runs out in a puffing hurry. Between warpath Indians and Dub Kreeger's gang, Robert's Station is nothing but a mare's nest of trouble."

She mulled all this for a full minute, watching him. "There's something to what you say. But *if* . . . somebody knew where that payroll was, don't you agree it's just as easy to split it four ways as three?"

"So you're dealing me in and Crazy Charlie out."

"Charlie?" she repeated, the word dripping scorn. "He don't mean spit. As long as he's got a nose to pick, he has no use for gold."

Fargo shook his head. "It'll be split, all right, among officers and men of the U.S. Army. It belongs to them."

Darlene stamped her shapely little foot. "Set it to a tune! Do you think the U.S. Army gives a hoot about Skye Fargo?"

"You joshing? I know a few officers who'd like to throw a necktie party for me."

"Married officers, I'll bet."

Fargo stood mute for she was right.

"So who gives a damn," she persisted, "about the army? They'll replace that gold. And since they think it was stolen, they'll blame Dub Kreeger. Fargo, four ways—we'll all be rich."

"Yeah, and then what's the difference between us and Dub Kreeger?"

"Oh, what's got into you—religion? That high-road crap ain't your style, Fargo."

Fargo nodded agreement. "Yeah, but you're forgetting Captain Jasper Dundee."

"The fellow that was killed? What about him?"

"For one thing, blood vengeance. I don't budge from here until I kill Kreeger and his bunch. For another, we were both sent up here to rescue you ladies and find out about that gold. If I file a false report, I'm doing dirt on an honest soldier."

"Oh, stuff! Let me run get some water so you can baptize me! Fargo, you don't fool me for one minute. All this psalm singing is just to cover your own plan for stealing the gold. Meantime, you intend to screw my sisters to keep yourself entertained."

Fargo grinned. "Three would make a whole set."

Her eyes shot sparks at him. "You filthy horned toad! I wouldn't spread my legs for you if you were a midwife! Go out in the barn with that other filthy hyena!"

Fargo called it a good morning's work. He had all but confirmed that Darlene, at least, knew where the payroll was.

47

"I'm going," he promised. "But I expect gunplay the moment I go out this door. Give me just one minute to get ready. And grab your Volcanic—this might be your chance to kill some of the men trying to snatch that gold from you."

He returned to the cubbyhole out back and fished his spare buckskins out of his saddle pockets. He had already carried an armful of straw from the stock barn the night before. He stuffed his shirt and trousers with the straw.

"What in the world do you want with a scarecrow?" Darlene demanded when he returned.

"I call it a buckskin man," Fargo explained as he jammed a picket pin into the straw at the neck of the shirt and hung his hat on it. "Hand me that broom."

Fargo pried the end of the broom handle up under the back of the shirt.

"All right," he told Darlene, "rack that gun and get over to a loophole. I'll wager all hell will break loose the second I open this door and shove this straw Fargo outside. Watch for their powder smoke and then pour the lead to 'em."

Fargo already had his Henry propped against the front wall. The light slanting through the loopholes told him it was past sunup. Staying behind the angle of the door, he threw it open and thrust the buckskin man out.

Even knowing it was coming, the hammering racket of gunfire made Fargo wince. Four Spencer carbines opened up, the big slugs shredding the decoy and biting chunks out of the wood of the station house. Fargo's hat went spinning off, and one round nicked his beard.

"There!" he told Darlene, spotting feathers of black smoke from a clutch of boulders up the slope. "Straight above us!"

But Darlene had already spotted them. She opened up with the Volcanic as Fargo dropped the straw man and snatched up his Henry, opening fire. Now six long guns were speaking their deadly peace, shattering the stillness of the mountain and echoing down through the canyons. Because of all the rocks and boulders, the long, tight whine of ricochets added to the chaos.

"They're starting to rabbit!" Fargo called out. "Make it hot for 'em, lady!"

The running men were exposed only briefly, but Fargo dropped a bead on a skinny man in a rawhide vest and squeezed off a round. The outlaw suddenly spun in his tracks, then recovered his footing and disappeared over the ridge with the others.

"You got one!" Darlene exclaimed.

"Looks like I only winged him," Fargo said, disappointed. "But there's no doctors around here, and even a minor wound can send a man under. Good shooting, Darlene. You had those rat bastards ducking for cover."

She studied Fargo closely as he pulled his tattered straw man back inside. "That stuff they write about you ain't just humbug, is it? You made them fools waste ammunition and show us where they was holed up."

Fargo glanced ruefully at his bullet-riddled buckskins. "I s'pose. But now I have to patch my duds."

Sharlene's frightened voice drifted out of the bedroom. "Christ on a crutch! What in blazes is going on?"

Darlene ignored her, still watching Fargo. "Think about it. A four-way split. And if you stayed with us after we leave, you'd have the whole set—anytime you wanted."

Fargo measured out a long sigh, thinking: *pile on the agony.* Out loud he said only, "If I was ever tempted."

"If you're tempted," Darlene reasoned, "then just do it."

The Flathead war chief named Spotted Pony watched the blazing gun battle below with great satisfaction.

"These white dogs," he told the shaman Tangle Hair, "war with each other and make our task easier. But their thunder sticks make more noise than they do widows. Only one man was wounded although perhaps someone in the lodge was also struck."

"No," Tangle Hair said. "The lodge is still protected by the ghosts of those recently killed."

Spotted Pony held his face expressionless in the warrior way and said nothing to this. Many in the tribe set great store by Tangle Hair's pronouncements. But Spotted Pony remembered the time when Tangle Hair blessed each brave's medicine bundle before a fight with buffalo hiders near the Paha Sapa, known as the Black Hills to white eyes. The shaman swore that the paleface bullets would be turned to sand. Yet, four braves had been killed and ten more wounded before Spotted Pony was forced to show the white feather.

"These ghosts," Spotted Pony finally said. "They are hair-faced ghosts, not red ghosts. Why would their magic be the same as ours?"

"Ask the Great Supernatural this thing. It is His will, not mine."

Spotted Pony could still see dark smoke curling over the rocky slope below. "It is His will, yet you somehow know it? Just as you know how to turn bullets into sand?"

This was near heresy, and Spotted Pony would not speak these words in front of witnesses. But his band of twenty warriors was camped about a mile back, behind the shoulder of the mountain.

"My medicine is strong," Tangle Hair protested. "But sometimes an enemy can place a false vision over a shaman's eyes, and he believes it is true."

"So you told the council after the hiders drove us off. And thus you were spared. But a war leader who loses so many braves is severely punished. I was forced to put up a pole and hang for a full sleep by hooks. Do you know what that pain is like?"

Tangle Hair folded his arms to show his disapproval of this talk. "You are a warrior and a battle leader. It is your fate to take pain."

Spotted Pony held his strong face as stiff as granite. "I have ears for these words. Just as it is your fate to eat and grow soft, to take your pick of our young women. And to fall back when the battle cry sounds."

"Spotted Pony, I know you are eager to attack this strange lodge. But only think: you cannot let your zeal for the fight overcome your obligations to the Day Maker and your medicine man. Think of the Cheyenne and the Lakota, the Arapaho. These tribes are still formidable because they cling to the magic and beliefs of their past. Now think of the tribes down in the desert country who have forsaken their gods to worship the white man's. They are slaves who believe a virgin had a baby, and now they grow corn like women."

Spotted Pony did think on all this. One rebellious part of

50

his heart wanted to kill Tangle Hair and reject his magic. But another part, the greater part, knew the elder was right. An Indian lived only through the tribe.

"You have spoken words I can place in my parfleche," he finally said. "But that lodge is what keeps hair-faces on this new road. We must kill every paleface inside it and burn it to the ground. These ghosts you insist protect it—they had better leave soon."

9

Moving quickly to frustrate any snipers, Fargo crossed to the stock barn. To his surprise he found Crazy Charlie leading one of the team horses up and down the barn, a saddle on its back.

"I haven't mounted him yet," the stock tender explained. "But he takes the bit now, and it won't be long before he's struttin' right alongside that fine pinto of yours."

"Good work, Charlie. But keep it up, and work fast. You heard that ruckus a while ago. Dub Kreeger is on the scrap and he's got a fire lit under him—he means to heist that gold."

"Ain't just him," Charlie remarked, digging in his nose with his free hand. "While you was tossing lead at them French-leave soldiers, Injins was watching."

Fargo alerted like a hound on point. "Watching from where?"

"A shelf about halfway up the mountain."

"Hunh. How many?"

"All I seen was two," Crazy Charlie replied, still walking the horse. "But I seen 'em before. They use to attack the station until we buried the girls' husbands. One's a heap big battle chief—had at least forty eagle tail feathers in his war bonnet. I figure the other one is a medicine man—he wore buffalo horns and had a mess of totems and such painted on his pony."

Fargo nodded, stroking his beard thoughtfully. "I got no idea who the medicine man is. But from what you say about that war bonnet, I'd bet my boots that's the Flathead war leader Spotted Pony. I hear tell he's double rough—went on the warpath when the Oregon Trail got to rolling good. He's trying to stir up the other tribes into a war of extermination against whites."

Crazy Charlie hooted. "Then he's a consarn red fool! Hell, the palefaces are wipin' themselves out at the most astounding rate. Them three planted behind the station wasn't popped over by Injins. No need for the red man to pitch into the game."

Fargo eyed him closely. "Tell the truth and shame the devil. Well spoken for a crazy man."

"Like I said, I'm crazy, not stupid."

"Uh-huh. Anyhow, we need to get those horses broke to the saddle mighty damn quick. We have a good defensive position here, but all these strikes are costing us ammo. Those Flatheads won't wait forever before they start attacking again."

"You're forgetting one thing," Charlie said, a wicked grin on his lips.

"Well, you got a fishbone caught in your throat? Spit it out."

"Them lovely ladies," Charlie said, "ain't goin' nowhere without that legem pone."

"So you admit they have it? Fess up."

"Ain't saying that, long-tall. Just saying they won't leave without it."

"I'm sorely tempted to thrash you," Fargo said. "All four of you, just as coy as a Saint Louis whore. Well, sell your ass. Darlene as much as admitted that she knows where the gold is. Tried to talk me into going snooks on it."

Charlie wagged a warning finger at Fargo. "I know Darlene, Fargo, and not just her fine tits. She ain't about to split with you, me, nor the Queen of England. That talk is just to lure you into helping them get outta here. Then she'll shoot you in the brainpan and let the buzzards bury you."

Fargo grinned. "You think I just fell off the turnip wagon? I know a calculating bitch when I see one."

Crazy Charlie tossed back his head and howled like a coyote.

"There was a cruel lass from Boston,
Who shot every man in Austin,
She'd say with a grin,
As her cylinder did spin,
'It forces me to move quite often.'"

Fargo shook his head and moved down to the Ovaro's stall. The stallion nuzzled his shoulder in greeting, clearly eager to shake out the night kinks. Charlie had been generous with the rubdowns and currycomb, and the stallion's coat was sleek and glossy.

Where, Fargo wondered yet again, would those sly little beauties hide that gold? Hiding it close to the station would of course be easier. But with Dub Kreeger and his cockroaches after it, not to mention any authorities who might come along, it might be more practical to hide it well away from the station. A small strongbox wasn't all that heavy, and two young women could easily carry it—especially if that conniving bastard Crazy Charlie was in the mix.

But was he? Fargo believed what Charlie said just a few minutes ago—that the sisters, especially Darlene, had no intention of sharing that stolen money with anyone, Charlie included. But did Charlie really believe that, or was the remark just lip deep?

Fargo measured out a long, fluming sigh, deeply regretting that he had taken on this job. Frankly, he didn't give a tinker's damn about the stolen gold, and he had no desire to lock horns with Flathead Indians—hell, they had their side of it too, and the hair-faces *were* encroaching on the red nations. Dub Kreeger's bunch, however, were a different kettle of fish. Jasper Dundee's new grave up in the high lonesome was a reminder that Fargo would definitely be huggin' with the snowbirds.

Fargo whistled the Ovaro out of its stall and grabbed his saddle from a nearby rack. He tossed on the pad, then centered the saddle over the stallion's back and took his bridle down from a nearby coffee can nailed to a support beam. The Ovaro easily took the bit and Fargo slipped the headstall over its ears before fastening the throat latch.

"You think it's smart to ride out?" Crazy Charlie asked, still walking the big team horse.

"Been a coon's age since I did anything smart," Fargo admitted. "Matter fact, I'm the dumbest son of a bitch in seventeen states. I keep working for the army."

"There's more than seventeen states now," Charlie piped up. "So you're not dumb everyplace you go."

"Never mind your foolishness," Fargo said brusquely as he cinched the girth. "I want you to keep your ears and eyes open. When they see me ride out, Kreeger and his yellow curs may try another strike on this place. Keep your rifle to hand."

"More likely they'll try to wipe you out of the saddle."

"Like I said," Fargo told him, leading the Ovaro out of the barn, "it's been a while since I did anything smart."

Fargo ducked into the station just long enough to warn the sisters to be on the qui vive. Before forking leather and riding out, he led his horse around to the small apron of tall grass behind the building. There was a rickety old jakes just beyond the dogtrot. Fargo shouldered the door open and found nothing but a wasp's nest and an old Winchester catalog, half its pages torn out.

Next he moved to the very lip of the drop-off about twenty yards past the three new graves. Below him was a sheer granite face, completely vertical and devoid of any hand- or footholds, falling for at least five hundred feet. Not only could it not be scaled, but the white-water stream roaring along the bottom left no room for caching anything.

There's still the girls' bedroom, Fargo thought idly as he led the Ovaro back into the yard and stepped up into leather. He strongly doubted the gold was hidden there—too easy to find. Still, he'd somehow take a look soon.

Before he broke into the open Fargo pulled out his field glasses and carefully studied the rocky slopes and crags rising above the federal road. He watched for movements, not shapes, and for reflections. If Kreeger's bunch was waiting to ambush him, they were doing a fine job of looking like parts of the mountain.

As he rode past the stock barn and the corral, Crazy Charlie's gravel-pan voice assaulted his ears:

"Old King Cole was a merry old soul,
With a deerskin belly and a rubber asshole!"

Fargo's lips twitched into a grin. But he wondered, yet again, just how "crazy" the man really was.

"Well, there below goes the great crusader, chappies," Dub Kreeger announced. "If we had a Big Fifty and crossed sticks to steady it, I'd spray his brains all over that new road."

Kreeger watched their new enemy in silence for a few moments, then laid his field glasses aside. "That bastard rooked us good with them stuffed buckskins. He's trickier than a redheaded woman, but a tricky man dies just as hard as all the rest."

"With him it ain't the dying I worry about," Fats Munro said between hissing intakes of painful breath. "It's the killing will be the hard part. My left shoulder feels like there's a red-hot poker in it."

"Quitcher bitchin'," Willy Hanchon told Fats. "He only winged you. Fargo will deal us worse misery than that if we don't burn him down quick. That son of a bitch is death to the devil."

"People talk him up mighty big," Dub said, picking up the glasses to again watch the man riding far below—too far to open up on. "And Fargo is a hard twist—that's no shit. But he's up to the hubs in bad trouble. He's got us, savages greased for war, and them three wildcats to whip. It's root hog or die for Skye goddamn Fargo. This time, boys, he's stepped in something he can't wipe off."

"It ain't exactly a Sunday school picnic for us, neither," Fats said.

"No? Well we're sittin' on enough ammunition to last us a year. The savages ain't got a gun between 'em, and with enough raids we'll force Fargo, the idiot, and the high-toned whores to run out. We're sittin' in the catbird seat, boys, and I can smell that gold already."

"*Damn* but this shoulder is giving me jip," Fats interjected. "You ought to've flushed it with liquor, Dub. I'm thinkin' it might putrefy."

"Take the pain like a man," Kreeger snarled. "Christ, it's a long way from your heart. We ain't got enough old orchard to waste on that flea bite. I told you the bullet went through, and the wound is tied off. The hell you want, egg in your beer?"

Barrel-chested Link Jeffries scowled at this last remark. The dimwit was in a foul mood, most of it directed at this new interloper in buckskins.

"Eggs and beer?" he said sarcastically. "We ain't seen neither in the best part of a year. I've et so much salt pork I'm commencing to oink. Hell, for some reason the savages has pulled back, and we was all set to corral them women and make off with that gold. Then along comes this cockchafer Fargo. It makes me wrathy, boys, wrathy as a sore-tailed bear."

He clenched and unclenched his ham-sized fists, and Dub took careful notice. Link was a good man in a scrape and, single-handedly, could free a horse mired in the mud. But he was unstable nitro and had to be handled carefully.

"Makes me wrathy too, Link," he said soothingly. "Hell, ever since I laid eyes on that Marlene, I got me a flagpole in my pocket. All I can think on is that little blond-haired cunny of hers. But we gotta be patient a while longer. Skye Fargo ain't what you call trifling danger."

"Winter comes early up here," Willy said. "Real early. If we fiddle-fuck around too much longer, the first snowfall will close the passes. That means we don't get out until spring thaw. Ain't none of us mountain men—we'll freeze to death in some damn cave."

"Buncha damn weak sisters," Dub muttered. "Well, stop frettin'. There's plenty of time until first snowfall, and we'll have that gold with time to spare—mark my words. Now let's grab leather and head down this slope—Fargo's poking real slow-like along the road, likely looking for that strong-box. If he goes far enough, we'll hit Robert's Station again. If he don't, mayhap we'll get a good bead on him."

"I want his horse," Fats spoke up. "That b'hoy put a Kentucky pill through my shoulder, and I got dibs on his stallion."

"Sure, Fats, that's how it should be," Dub said. But he had seen the inside of that bullet wound, and he knew damn good and well it was already putrefying. Within two or three days Fats would be worm fodder—and three men would share that gold instead of four. First, however, they had to clear the path of their main encumbrance: the Trailsman.

Fargo stuck to the well-graded federal road, giving the Ovaro his head and letting the stallion set the pace. The army engineers had done a good job of selecting a route that was mostly free of good ambush points except for the middle and far distances. Fargo knew the Spencer carbine, while a good repeating rifle, was not as effective beyond three hundred yards.

Then again, he reminded himself, one of those jackals had plugged Jasper Dundee at that distance. And it was not Fargo's way to assume it was just a lucky shot.

With such thoughts looping through his mind, he constantly scanned the right-hand side of the trail, the rocky slope leading up to the granite pinnacle of the mountain. The left-hand slope posed little danger: a few scraggly patches of jack pine dotting mostly open terrain covered with talus and broken shale. He was too high up into the Bitterroot Range to worry about trees or large bushes.

When he wasn't watching the slope, Fargo kept his eyes aimed at the ground to either side of the road. If the sisters had cached that strongbox away from Robert's Station, they would likely have stuck to the road. Nor would they have lugged it very far, not with Kreeger's gang and warpath Indians in the area.

Now and again he swung down to dismantle a heap of rocks or explore under a flat piece of shale. All he turned up was a buzzing rattlesnake that damn near sank its long fangs into his leg. Fargo killed it with his knife just in time to keep the Ovaro from spooking.

He was about two miles west of the station when the Ovaro's ears pricked forward.

"I was wondering when our friends would send in their calling card, old campaigner," he said quietly to his horse, patting it gently on the neck. "Just keep up the strut like nothing's happening."

Fargo cast quick, sidelong glances until he finally caught a flash of reflection about three hundred yards up the slope, an area obscured by boulders. It worried him. Even if he was still a hard target, the Ovaro wasn't.

"This is no time to stand and hold," he told his mount. "I can't afford to waste ammo. Let's vamoose!"

Fargo quickly wheeled the Ovaro and thumped him with his heels. "Hi-ya!" he shouted. "Gee up, old warhorse!"

The Ovaro had been impatiently waiting for a chance to stretch it out. Even as the first carbines began cracking, the stallion had lowered himself and begun lengthening his strides, ears pinned back. Fargo lowered himself, too, shifting much of his body to the cover of the Ovaro's right flank.

Bullets pockmarked the road and snapped past Fargo's ears with a sound like angry hornets. One nicked his saddle fender only inches from his leg. As they finally drew out of range, Fargo made up his mind. The cat-and-mouse game these dry-gulching bastards obviously preferred could only end in disaster for Fargo and the other defenders at Robert's Station.

It was time to play by the Trailsman's rules.

It was time to take the bull by the horns.

10

When Fargo returned to Robert's Station, he caught a whiff of hot biscuits and felt his digestive gears churning. Marlene answered his knock, her face both surprised and relieved when she saw him.

"We heard the racket down the road and figured you for a goner," she explained, closing the door behind him and pulling in the latch.

"Oh, there was a game afoot," Fargo replied, "but this time I won. Or anyhow, didn't lose."

"Had to be Kreeger and his bunch," Marlene said. "The Indians hereabouts ain't got no guns."

"Yeah, it was the courageous deserters. And they've got enough ammo to toss at the birds."

Darlene and Sharlene were seated at the trestle table, eating breakfast. Fargo could tell from their sullen faces that they'd been arguing and he bit back a sarcastic remark—it was no mystery who they were arguing about.

"Push those long legs under the table," Sharlene said, sparing a smile for Fargo. "We saved you a plate."

"I reckon both of you got a good appetite," Darlene said from a deadpan while Marlene darted into the kitchen for Fargo's plate.

"Me, I feel fit as a fiddle," Sharlene taunted her sister. "How 'bout you, Skye?"

"Slept the sleep of the just," Fargo replied as he folded his legs under the table.

"That's just plumb grand," Darlene interjected. "Better than a tonic. Louder, too. Sharlene, you made enough racket to wake snakes."

"Maybe I scared the Indians off."

Marlene returned with a plate of biscuits covered with honey. She also set down a pottery mug filled with coffee.

"Smells mighty good," Fargo said, tying into the food. "By the way, how you ladies set for provisions?"

"The larder is lighter," Sharlene quipped. "We got flour for a few more days, a sack of pinto beans, and some beef packed in lard—not much, though. We got about a pound of coffee beans but no more sugar. We use to have milk but the redskins killed our cow."

"They think cows are jack buffalos," Fargo said around a mouthful of food. "They kill them on sight so they won't mix with the buff herds."

Fargo suddenly felt a stab of guilt. "What about Crazy Charlie—does he have food?"

"I took him out a plate earlier," Marlene said. "We can't stand to watch him eat. He chews with his mouth open and belches real loud. Picks his teeth, too."

"He's making progress on saddle-breaking a couple of those team horses," Fargo said, his eyes meeting Darlene's. "Won't be long and we can light out from here."

"It'd be smarter," she replied, "to drive Dub Kreeger's gang out first. Even better if we could kill them."

"You and me," Fargo said, "have tied our thoughts to the same hitching post. The problem is firepower. We've got pretty good weapons, but dwindling ammo. Kreeger's bunch can reload ten to one on us."

"Yes, but you're a better shot. You wounded one this morning at quite a distance."

Fargo conceded the point with a nod. "The way he twisted, I think it was a good score. And since outlaws don't give a damn about their own, with luck the one I hit is dead or dying."

Darlene warmed to her theme. "Mm-hm. We *have* to kill them while we're here in the station or they'll ravish all three of us on the trail."

Fargo laid his fork down. "That's the straight word, and I don't take that threat lightly. But you're just blowing smoke, Darlene. What's really got you all consternated is fear for that gold. You need me to kill the Kreeger gang so they won't take it. And since you don't trust me any farther than you can throw me, you mean to murder me when you've had your use of me."

"If she does," Sharlene cut in, emerald eyes snapping sparks, "I swear I'll kill *her*!"

"If I don't do it first," chimed in Marlene. "Mr. Fargo is the bravest, handsomest man I ever met!"

"Thank you, dear," Fargo said, swallowing the praise effortlessly.

"You're right, Fargo," Darlene blazed. "Unlike my pea-brained sisters I *don't* trust you. But if—*if*—we had that gold, there'd be no need to kill you if you'd just throw in with us."

Fargo waved this suggestion aside. "I'm a stubborn man, so you can stifle that idea. But you're dead-on right about one thing: we'd be fools to hit that trail with the gang still alive. We'll likely have enough trouble with the feather-heads. You girls need to talk it over and come to Jesus about that gold. Don't forget, I can get you that recovery fee of twenty-eight hundred dollars. That's a nice pile of wampum."

If Fargo was stubborn, he had met his match in Darlene. Her pretty face suddenly closed like a book. "Gold? *What* gold, Mr. Fargo?"

Fargo, moving quickly to reduce his target, went out to the stock barn. Crazy Charlie had just finished rubbing down the Ovaro and leading him back into his stall.

"I walked him up and down to cool him out, just like you told me," he greeted Fargo. "He was lathered pretty good."

"'Preciate it," Fargo said, retrieving Jasper Dundee's saddlebags from the can where he'd hung them. "You been keeping an eye out for trouble?"

"That's mostly what I do anymore. I ain't seen nothing of a dangersome nature yet today. It's them dang red arabs I fret the most. Kreeger and his bunch will just shoot me if they see the chance. But the Flatheads will make a leather pouch out of a white man's scrotum, and they prefer to cut it off while he's screaming. Only outlanders peddle that Noble Red Man claptrap."

"I've met a few that are noble," Fargo gainsaid, "and some tribes that behave better than most whites I've met out west. The Plains warriors learned scalping from the Spanish, and it's white trappers and traders that gave 'em a taste for fire-water."

"You're no Indian lover, Fargo. You've sent plenty to the Land of Ghosts, ain't you?"

Fargo nodded. "There's blood in their eyes now, and a man has to defend himself. This bunch under Spotted Pony ain't your thirty-five cent warriors. They've all counted coup, killed an enemy, and been bloodied in battle. These are the hardest of the hard twists. They've held back because there's a hoodoo on this place—fresh-dead white men whose souls are floating around, waiting to jump into the first body they see, red or white. But a bravo like Spotted Pony won't stay his hand much longer. And when they strike, we best have some powerful medicine."

Charlie hadn't missed a word of this. "By Saint Barbara! To hear you tell it, we're all gone beavers."

"Clean your ears or cut your hair, crazy man. I'm just telling you the truth about Ruth. Powerful medicine, that's the ticket. With us running low on ammo, we got to switch tactics. It's best to surprise, mystify, and confuse your enemy. That holds true whether it's red marauders or white."

"Tactics? That's your bailiwick, Mr. Fargo. I'm a simple shit who howls at the moon."

Fargo tossed the saddlebags onto a workbench and watched the stock tender, narrowing his eyes. "That's what you keep saying. You know, old son, a man can't fake being fat nor tall nor skinny. But he can fake being crazy."

"A man would have to be crazy to do that."

"Uh-huh. Or wily. Anyhow, what do you know about gunpowder?"

Charlie began cavorting and singing:

"On the other side of France,
They don't wear any pants,
But they do wear grass
To cover up their—"

"Bottle it," Fargo snapped, digging something out of the bags. "I asked you what you know about gunpowder."

Crazy Charlie lifted one shoulder. "The Chinee invented

it, it clumps easy in damp weather, it makes a humdinger of a boom when you stuff it into a cannon."

"These are called blasting cans," Fargo explained, showing him two dull yellow cans with orange fuses protruding from the tops. "There's no shrapnel in these cans—just black powder. Army engineers use them to blow away ridges and rock piles. We've got four of them."

Charlie stared nervously at them. "Would one of these blow up this barn?"

Fargo shook his head. "Prob'ly set it on fire, but the blast radius isn't that big. It does make one helluva catarumpus when it goes off, though, and the black-powder smoke will turn day into night. To a savage that hasn't been around a white man's big-thundering weapons, it looks like heap big magic. I sent thirty Cheyenne Dog Soldiers screaming with one of these, and they're no boys to mess with."

"I take your drift," Charlie said, still watching the cans as if they were coiled snakes. "But Dub Kreeger's bunch were soldiers, they know about 'em."

"It's likely. But a blast close enough could kill or wound, and I'll double-dog guarantee their horses would scatter to the directions in a panic. I'll leave two in the barn with you since you got that loft door for good throwing. But *don't* waste them—only toss one if you're sure it will take good effect. And save one for the savages."

"What about the two you're keeping?"

"One is for the red sons."

Charlie studied Fargo's weather-bronzed face, searching for a clue to the Trailsman's plan. "And the other?"

Again Fargo reminded himself how this hunkering down strategy didn't fit his theory of warfare. Whether it was a large army or a beleaguered group like this one at Robert's Station, defensive combat usually simply delayed the inevitable defeat. A man had to take the fight to the enemy and keep the element of surprise on his side.

"The other one," he finally replied, "will soon kiss the mistress."

11

Fargo rolled into his blankets early on that second night at Robert's Station, knowing he had to hit the steep mountain slope well before sunrise. He also knew he'd have to ride shank's mare—a mounted rider on that shale-littered terrain would raise a clatter and turn himself into an easy target. This mission would require all the skills he'd acquired as a dismounted scout, and a fair ration of luck, too.

Despite the need to roll out early, he grinned when he heard a knock at the door. It had to be Sharlene or Marlene, and he was voting for the latter—untasted fruit was always the most tempting.

"Mr. Fargo?"

Fargo's grin melted like a snowflake on a river. It was Darlene's voice, and it didn't sound amorous. "Yeah?" he called to her.

"I just want to let you know that you won't be getting any visitors tonight. I got my sisters on a tight leash now."

"You're the one who's a dog off her leash," Fargo growled.

"And maybe if I was to come in there, you'd tame this dog, huh?"

"Some bitches are too mean to gentle."

He heard her goading laugh. "Too mean for the famous Trailsman? You must be going puny, cocksman. Or am I that ugly?"

"All right," Fargo said, "quit your grinnin' and drop your linen. I'll put the latch out and you can come on in. Tomorrow you'll be lipping salt out of my hand."

Again the goading laugh. "I don't give it away to every down-at-the-heels drifter like my sisters do. But I'll tell you what: change your thinking on this gold situation, and I'll send the girl of your choice. Or both at once."

Fargo perked up. "How about all three at once?"

"My lands, you *are* a dreamer," she replied. "But change your mind and you'll have us."

Fargo sat up in the cot, mulling this potential windfall. He could just lie, screw the living hell out of all three and . . . No, he decided, Darlene would shoot him dead as last Christmas. All right, he could throw in with them and help them steal the gold, filing a phony report at Fort Seeley. After all, with Jasper dead there was no other witness.

But Fargo cursed when he realized he couldn't do that. He was a jobber, not a scoundrel, and he couldn't do dirt on an employer like that. Besides, Captain Jasper Dundee died for this mission, and Fargo owed him good and faithful service.

"Darlene, if I was ever tempted," he replied on a sigh. "But I'm dealing this one from the top of the deck."

"Oh, up yours, you lily-livered Lancelot!" she snapped before she left. "Crazy Charlie has more gumption than you!"

Fargo's grin returned when he realized he had shattered her sneer of cold command. The woman had gold fever, just as bad as prospectors in the Sierra or on the Comstock. That made her dangerous—maybe just as dangerous as the curs he planned to visit tomorrow.

It was still dark when Fargo threw back his blanket and slapped his bare feet onto the cold, rammed-earth floor. He fired up the lamp, dressed quickly, and palmed the wheel of his Colt to check the loads. Reluctantly he decided to leave his Henry up in the main building with the sisters. The long barrel made it deadly accurate but also cumbersome for climbing and close-in work.

He opened a saddlebag and pulled out one of the blasting cans, carefully trimming the fuse shorter. Then he stuffed it into his possibles bag, doused the lamp, and went into the station house.

"Morning," Marlene greeted him. She was on guard duty and stood at one of the loopholes, lever-action Volcanic in her hands. "Coffee?"

Fargo shook his head, unable to pry his eyes away from the shapely blonde. Her thin blue cotton dress clung like an apple skin to her ample curves.

"Thanks, but I have to get thrashing. Here's an extra rifle. Depending on what happens up on the slope today, you gals might have a visit from Dub Kreeger. Remember, ammo is getting scarce, so don't shoot at rovers."

"What *is* going to happen up there, Skye?"

"I can't say. But with luck you'll be hearing a loud blast."

Her face lit up at this, but when she spoke her tone was serious. "I know a man like you is always careful, but watch that bunch. The way Dub Kreeger stares at me, I always feel like I need a bath."

"It's pretty hard not to stare at a girl like you. You're pretty as four aces and nature has been mighty kind to the rest of you, too."

She flushed with pleasure. "I don't mind when *you* look at me. Tell you the truth, I'm thinking the same thing you are."

Fargo removed his hat and discreetly moved it in front of his fly to cover his reaction to her candor. "But according to Darlene, she's got you and Sharlene on a tight leash around me."

"Well, *you* ain't on nobody's leash. Don't keep me waiting too long, Skye. Sharlene told me what it's like doing it with you, and it took my breath away."

Marlene quaffed the lamp long enough for Fargo to open the door and get outside without being backlit. The high-mountain air was crisp before sunrise and the black-velvet dome of sky peppered silver with stars. Up in the craggy pinnacles, the wind howled with a sound like souls in torment.

Fargo had guessed, from terrain features and ambush points, the probable area up on the steep slope where the gang had made camp. He moved down the federal road for a thousand yards or so, gnawing on a gnarled hunk of jerky. Then he veered onto the slope and started climbing.

The grade was steep, the footing uncertain especially in predawn darkness under a weak crescent of butter-colored moon. Eons of rock slides had sent scree and glacial moraine tumbling down the mountain, and Fargo had to test each foothold before he put his weight down. Much of the rock cover was jagged-edged, and he was grateful for the triple-soled boots he'd bought from a sutler back in Missouri.

He also had special-made footgear back in his saddlebags, light boots made of sponge and rubber that he sometimes used when scouting in close among vigilant Indians. But they would have been shredded to chair stuffings on this hostile surface.

At times the steep slope leveled out a bit, and the rock floor gave way to wild columbine and sparse gamma grass. Then Fargo would pause to catch his breath and listen. He also smelled deeply of the air, for he had learned to detect the odor of horses—and unwashed human bodies—from a great distance.

So far, nothing. He estimated he was halfway up the mountain and expected to have reached sight of the outlaw camp by now. The eastern sky was salmon pink with the promise of the new sunrise and time was rapidly dwindling. Daylight concealment would be difficult on this slope devoid of large boulders, and the Trailsman knew he would have to pull foot before very long.

"Pile on the agony," he muttered as he set off again.

He had clambered another fifty yards or so toward the summit when he spotted orange flames sawing in the stiff breeze.

Fargo hooked to the right, for he wanted to get above the camp. He searched everywhere, as he maneuvered, for their horses—if he could kill them and maroon these men afoot, that was their death warrant. No remounts were available in this lonely mountain region, and men on foot—especially outlaws with poor trailcraft—would soon be shoveling coal in hell.

But Fargo quickly realized these particular outlaws weren't as careless as most. They had taken pains to hide their horses well away from the camp. Which meant Fargo would have to rely on the blasting can and his Colt repeater.

Hunched low and moving carefully, he moved into position above the camp. They had also taken the precaution of standing guard through the night: He spotted a huge bear of a man with muscular arms sitting on a rock close to the fire.

Link Jeffries, Fargo told himself, remembering Jasper Dundee's descriptions of the gang.

A strained voice suddenly startled Fargo.

"Link? Link, ain't there anymore of that laudanum? I'm in a world of hurt here, boy."

"You done sucked all of it up, Fats," Jeffries replied in a bored voice. "You'll hafta be a man and take the pain."

"There's more! I *can't* take the pain, don'tcha see? It's gone from my shoulder into my neck and chest. Christ Jesus, I'm all swole up! The pizen's eatin' at me something awful."

Fargo couldn't see the man except for one boot, but it had to be Fats Munro. The one he wounded two days ago. Clearly he was on the feather edge of death, which meant the gang was trimmed down to three. Just as clear, he was suffering, but Fargo thought about Jasper's brains exploding in a spray from his head and felt no pity for this scum bucket.

A third voice, sleepy and irritated, chimed in from behind a bulwark of rocks.

"Will you two females quit battin' your gums? Christsakes, it ain't even light yet."

"I'm hurtin' real bad, Dub," Fats said in a querulous whine. "There's a right smart of pain. Link won't give me no more of the laudanum."

"That's on account I told him not to. Square up to it like a man, Fats. You're a gone coon. We can't waste it on a dead man."

"You always did give me the little end of the horn. All you had to do was pour some forty-rod into the wound, but you wouldn't spare a sup to save my life. It hurts, goddamn it! It hurts somethin' powerful!"

"It hurts bad, you say? You want some medicine? *Here's* a pill for what ails you, nancy boy."

A six-gun barked, and the echoing crack broke the morning silence.

"That white-livered son of a bitch," Dub Kreeger's voice said. "Old Fats was some pumpkins in a shooting frolic, but he lost his oysters as soon as Fargo tagged him. Link, drag the body off a piece, wouldja? That pus stinks like a whorehouse at low tide."

Fargo, hidden as best he could behind a heap of talus,

watched the big man pick up Fats—who was actually skinny enough to walk through a rake—as if he were a sack of feathers. He carried the body about forty yards away and dumped it unceremoniously into a rock cleft. By now the new day was getting dangerously light, and Fargo had to reach a decision.

He could easily gun down Link, but Dub and the man named Willy Hanchon were out of sight behind protective rocks. Once Fargo opened up, the other two would also open fire and force Fargo to rabbit. Killing two of the gang was a good start, but would the blasting can be more effective? It might not kill outright, but the huge flash was hot and could burn all three of them so severely they would end up like Fats, dying of infection.

Fargo decided on the can. He waited until Link returned and settled in by the fire. Fargo was fairly close, but it was going to be a tricky throw. The steep angle of the slope, and a parapet of rock arching over the camp, forced him to an exact toss—he would have to loft the can in high and drop it in with close precision.

He practiced the toss mentally, then scratched a lucifer to life on his boot and lit the fuse. But a second after the can went airborne, disaster struck. A sudden, strong gust of wind caught the can and drifted it an inch or two to the left—just enough to strike the parapet with a loud clang and send it ricocheting back at Fargo.

The Trailsman, adept at instant decisions in a crisis, sized this one up in an eyeblink. He could hope the fuse was long enough for him to catch the can and pitch it back in. But Link Jeffries was already drawing his six-gun, and Fargo would likely be shot before he made the second toss.

Which left only one other choice. Fargo whirled around on one heel, took three long bounds, then lowered himself and dove forward like a man diving into water, not sharp rocks. He broke the dangerous landing with his arms braced, feeling pain explode throughout his body. The moment he landed a powerful blast behind him tossed rocks like chaff and sent searing heat licking over him.

"It's Fargo!" a voice bellowed behind him. "Put at him, boys!"

Wincing at the pain, but grateful he wasn't confetti, Fargo

pushed to his feet and immediately hooked around to the right to escape down the slope. Bullets whanged in all around him, ricocheting from rock to rock with a screaming whine. Fargo knocked the thong off the hammer of his Colt and cleared leather, snap-shooting toward his enemy without aiming.

Shooting wouldn't get him out of this scrape. Six bullets could only buy him a little time, and if he stopped to load his spare cylinder he'd be dead in a finger snap. Instinct told him that only speed—reckless, hell-bent-for-election speed—would keep him among the living. So Fargo gritted his teeth and threw all caution to the wind on this steep and treacherous slope.

With bullets nipping at his heels and fanning his ears, he focused his experienced eyes on the slope and leaped like a mountain goat from rock to rock. He had studied this kind of mountain terrain over the years with the attention of a scientist, and he guessed which flat pieces of shale or granite would hold him and which would send him ass over applecart. But at this breakneck speed, one misjudgment could send him in a tumbling death roll clear to the bottom, taking along a ton of rocks for his tomb.

"Air him out, goddamn it!" came a fading shout from behind him.

Six-guns and army carbines cracked with a noise like an ice floe breaking apart, and Skye Fargo hurtled downward with his heart in his throat.

12

"He musta been killed," Darlene announced near midmorning. "You heard that blast and then all that gunfire. He only took one gun with him, so it sure's hell wasn't Fargo doing all that shooting."

"It was him made the blast," Marlene argued. "He told me he was going to."

"Oh, ain't *he* the rip-staver?" Darlene barbed. "Made a big blast, my, my. Well if that big blast done any good, who done all the shootin' afterward? Pretty lively show for dead men."

"You're disgusting," Sharlene put in. "You don't give a hang about his life. You just want him to kill the Kreeger gang so you can haul that gold outta here."

"Well, ain't much hope of that now, is there? The big hero of the newspapers and nickel novels bit off more than he could chew. Now we're stuck with a halfwit who picks his nose and ogles our tits. We're up Salt River now, girls. Least we got another good horse and a rifle and ammo."

Each of the three sisters stood in front of a loophole, waiting for the attack Fargo had hinted might come.

"He ain't dead," Marlene said stubbornly. "It went bad up there, but he'll be back."

"Yes, you hope so, don't you?" Darlene said. "Ever since Sharlene told you about his big pecker, you been horny for him."

"So? And I s'pose you ain't?"

"I wouldn't mind strapping him on," Darlene admitted. "And I was going to if it meant getting shut of this place. He's a fine specimen of manhood, and I ain't never heard Sharlene howl like she done with him. But a woman's pussy is just a tool to get a job done. Don't matter now anyhow. Kreeger's bunch has sent him over the mountains."

"You ain't got no romance in your soul, Darlene," Marlene scolded. "*My* valentine ain't no tool. It's for pleasure, not work. And he'll be back, you'll see."

"Yes, every Jack shall have his Jill, too. And oysters will walk upstairs. Christ, Marlene, shut pan and flush out your headpiece. We're in a powerful fix here, and we gotta figure some way to wangle out of it. If we pull this off, there'll be no more hog and hominy on *our* plates. But time is a bird, sis, and that bird is on the wing."

"Here's Skye!" Sharlene cut in excitedly. "Or what's left of him. My lands, he looks like he just crawled off a battle-field!"

Marlene sprang to the door and Fargo limped into the station, a frightful sight. His buckskins were torn at the elbows and knees, revealing scraped and bloody skin. The back of his hair was singed, as was the brim of his plainsman's hat.

"The legend returns," Darlene said in a sarcastic voice. "Where's your scalps?"

Fargo dropped heavily onto one of the benches and shot her a warning glance. "Yours would fetch a good price, beauty."

"We figured you for dead," Sharlene said, pouring some water into a cup for him. "Or anyhow, Darlene did."

"Take your shirt off and pull them trousers up," Marlene said. "I'll wash and dress them wounds."

"Yes, let's see those battle scars," Darlene goaded. "Let me guess. You done your damnedest, but the gang was too much. Now maybe you figure to take all that gold yourself because it's easier for one man on a good horse to get away. And of course you mean to return it to the army."

"How could such a fine-looking woman," Fargo mused, "be so full of shit? Gold lust has turned you into a real piece of work, Darlene."

"Well, you did come a cropper up on that slope, didn't you?"

"The way you say. But I don't enlist for the battle—I'm in it to win it, and that means the whole war. I'll be huggin' with the Kreeger bunch again, count on it."

Marlene returned with soap, water, alum powder, and linen dressings. Even Darlene couldn't help staring in wonder when Fargo pulled off his shirt, a sea change coming over her face. The corded muscles of his chest, back, and shoulders were pockmarked with old knife and bullet wounds and several lumps of burn scar.

"Would you call *those* battle scars?" Sharlene demanded of her older sister.

Darlene let her silence answer the question.

"Did you kill any of them, Skye?" Marlene asked as she rinsed off a bloody elbow.

"The one I wounded was shot by Dub Kreeger. The wound festered and he was a gone-up case."

"Which one?" Darlene demanded.

"The one called Fats."

"He was a mean one, all right," Darlene said, her tone satisfied. "Too bad it wasn't Dub. But it's a start."

Her mood had visibly improved after seeing the record of Fargo's hard life impressed in his skin. A man who has survived all that, her manner seemed to say, was mighty useful to three women in a bind.

"This is no time to recite coups," Fargo warned. "It's likely those three will answer my attack with one of their own. I'm going over to the stock barn to make sure Crazy Charlie is sober. You gals keep a sharp eye out. And remember, hoard those bullets. Don't bust a cap unless you've got a good chance to score. And don't aim at the men—the horses are a bigger target. I don't cotton to killing horses, but this bunch are savage as a meat axe and well supplied with cartridges. Either we bend with the breeze or we break."

Fargo moved quickly to the stock barn and spotted Charlie in the paddock, riding the fully tacked roan with the blazed forehead. He waved to Fargo.

"Gentle enough to carry a baby!" he called out. "First combination horse I ever trained, and it was easy as rolling off a log. You were right as rain, Fargo. These pulling horses got no meanness in 'em—they just have to get used to the tack and some simple commands."

"A job well done, old son," Fargo called back. "But we'll

need two more pronto. The Kreeger gang is trouble, all right, but there's only three left and they got chicken shit for guts. It's the Flathead war party we need to avoid, and they won't stay their hands for long."

As Fargo drew closer, Crazy Charlie did a double take at the bloody buckskins. "I *knew* it when I heard the explosion this morning. You tossed a blasting can at the gang, hanh?"

"It musta been made of India rubber," Fargo quipped, "because it came bouncing back to me. Not exactly Fargo's finest hour."

Crazy Charlie tossed his head back and yipped like a coyote. Then he broke into one of his bawdy verses:

"In days of old when knights were bold,
And privies not invented,
They left their load
By the side of the road,
And walked away contented."

Fargo measured out a long sigh and shook his head. "Listen, you moonstruck fool, don't be capering around out here. That slope dead ahead of you could conceal Kreeger's men. An attack could come at any time. Come inside."

"I got to go out there later on," Charlie protested. "We're all damn near out of meat, and I got some snares set. We oughter have a few fat rabbits."

Charlie led the horse inside while Fargo retrieved Jasper Dundee's carbine and a bandolier.

"Can you shoot a Spencer?" Fargo asked him.

"Never have, boss. Itty-bitty little thing, ain't it?"

"Don't let size fool you. It fires a .56 caliber slug and it's a knock-down gun. It holds seven rounds, and you reload by opening this butt plate. All you do is lever and fire just like with my Henry. I'm leaving this and the ammo belt with you."

"But I got a good rifle."

Fargo nodded. "Damn good. But you have to jerk the bolt and insert each round. I want you to have something faster. I'm taking the captain's sidearm over to the station—that door is solid, but in case it gets breached I want them gals to have plenty of firepower."

75

At mention of the sisters, Charlie leered and cupped his hands in front of his scrawny chest. "Oh, they got firepower, indeedy-do! I wish to God I could be beat to death by them colossal catheads. Have you noticed how Sharlene's nipples—"

Fargo raised a hand to silence him. "All the fine tits in the world are useless to a man in the grave. Get them women off your mind, old son, and worry about two things: breaking them other two horses to leather and keeping your eyes peeled for an attack."

"All right," Charlie agreed without enthusiasm. "But I don't care one red cent about the *women*. They wouldn't piss in my ear if my brains was on fire. It's their tits I admire— just their tits. Like you said, *two things*."

Fargo narrowed his eyes and studied the stock tender for a long moment, his face speculative. "Charlie, you're not really crazy, are you?"

Crazy Charlie dug an index finger into his nose. "Depends when you ask."

Fargo averted his eyes in disgust. "It's all an act—a pretty good one, too. You know about that gold, don't you?"

"I know the girls took it, boss."

"Well, strike a light! First straight answer I've got around here. So where is it?"

"I don't know where they hid it. Honest to Christ I don't."

"You saw them take it?"

"Nuh-unh. But I spy through the loopholes a lot, hoping to glom some titties. And I hear things. Especially Darlene. Big talk about what they're gonna do when they bust out of here."

Fargo decided Charlie could be speaking straight arrow, but it was nothing that Darlene hadn't already implied in her attempts to bribe Fargo. He had searched the barn, part of the road, and the little rooms under the dogtrot. He had also searched the main room of the station house. The kitchen and their bedroom would have to be searched along with the roadway to the east.

The barn, Fargo suddenly thought. He had searched it, but not thoroughly enough. One bale of hay could hide a small payroll strongbox. And Fargo had not poked all of them. He didn't trust Charlie, and while the girls might actually control the swag, Charlie could be in it with them—why else would they put their tits on the glass for a man who so obviously disgusted them?

"All right," Fargo said just before he left the barn. "And for Christ sakes, get that finger outta your nose."

About midafternoon Fargo saw Crazy Charlie, rifle dangling from his left hand, head toward the scraggly terrain west of Robert's Station to check his snares. Fargo climbed up into the loft, slid the Arkansas toothpick from his boot, and began a more thorough search of the hay bales. Now and then he paused to look out the loft door, watching for movement on the mountain slope.

"Yoo-hoo!" came the lilting, musical voice from below. "Skye, are you here?"

Fargo sighed in baffled resignation. Warpath Indians and ruthless road agents he could understand and fight—it was lock horns and let the devil take the hindmost. But these three weird, beautiful sisters would neither go to church nor stay home. They needed him for protection but knew he was looking for the strongbox, and it was clear as a blood spoor in new snow they had that payroll—and meant to spend every last gold cartwheel. Marlene had been sweet to him, but was that part of Darlene's plan for controlling him?

"Up in the loft, Marlene," he called down as she entered the barn. "I'll come on down."

"You needn't bother," she said hastily. "It ain't modest for ladies to climb ladders in a dress, but I like . . . stretching out in hay, don't you?"

Her coy words resonated with layers of meaning. Fargo shook his head in wonder at these sly vixens. "Here we go again—ring around the rosy."

Her blond curls and perfect oval of face popped up over the floor of the loft. "Beg your pardon?"

Fargo lifted her the rest of the way into the loft. She felt light as a feather and brought a waft of lilac perfume with her. "Nothing, darlin'. Just muttering out loud."

She giggled. "I do that all the time. Now we got something in common. How's those wounds?"

"Fine thanks to you."

Fargo's glance swept over the sweet little frontier tidbit. She wore a faded but clean cotton dress that molded itself to her like a second skin. It was clear that, like her two older sisters, she wore no corset, chemise, or pantaloons underneath.

"It's safe to say you're not carrying a gun," Fargo said. "That's some consolation."

"No, but I got this." Marlene reached up to her neck and tugged at a silver chain Fargo thought was just a necklace. He recognized the small but sturdy obsidian-bladed weapon that popped into view: a Cheyenne Indian suicide knife. One was worn at all times by young Cheyenne women.

She said, "Addison—that was my husband—give it to me. Found it on a dead Cheyenne gal near the Black Hills. He said a Cheyenne squaw places her chas—chest—"

"Chastity," Fargo suggested.

She beamed at him. "The very word! You're handsome *and* smart. Anyhow, they're expected to kill themselves before they let a man . . . outage them. Is that right?"

"The way you say."

"Well, anyhow, I didn't want to disappoint Addison, but truth to tell, my chastity was gone long before us girls met him and his brothers. Heck, us girls started going off into the bushes with boys on our way home from Sunday school back in Pennsylvania."

"So why do you wear it?" Fargo asked.

Marlene kicked some loose hay into a pile and sat gracefully down. She patted the spot beside her and Fargo joined her.

"I wear it," she confided in a voice just above a whisper, "because Darlene told me to cut your throat with it. She told me to pull out your pecker and skin the cat with my hand until you get your shiver. You're a man, you know how it is when you get your shiver—you don't notice nothing but your pleasure."

Despite all he had witnessed of the Stanton sisters, Fargo was flat-out astounded by Marlene's frank confession. "I thought she intended to use me to kill off the Kreeger gang?"

"She did until she saw you with your shirt off—all them scars and such. That convinced her you're truly dangerous, not just some got-up hero in the newspapers. She's decided you *will* take the gold back."

"Well," he said, glancing at the knife again, "do you plan to slice my gullet?"

"'Course not, and Darlene don't really want you dead, neither. What she really wants is for you to put her ankles behind her ears and make her see God. Sharlene keeps battin' her gums about how you're hung like a stallion and know how to use it. But, see, Darlene is the most greedy for that gold."

"How 'bout you?"

She leveled her China blue eyes on him and batted her lashes. "Shucks, it's a heap of money, sure enough, and I want some of it."

"Marlene, where did you girls hide it?"

"Me and Sharlene didn't—Darlene did. She don't trust us and never has, nohow you could fix it. That's the gospel, Skye. But, see, it's *still* a heap of money even if we was to deal you in for a divvy. Seven thousand dollars—why, you could go into retiracy. You ever had that much money at one time, long-shanks?"

"Not any that I could legally keep. Which is true of this payroll, too."

Marlene made a cute little moue. "Legally? Skye, there's no real law west of the Missouri."

Fargo traced her finely sculpted cheekbones with one finger. "You're mighty easy on the eyes, honey, but you're at least half a bubble off plumb. You won't find right and wrong on a map. If *you* were a soldier waiting to get paid, would it still be hunky-dory for me to help steal that gold?"

"If *I* was a soldier, there'd be happy men in at least one barracks."

Fargo laughed, conceding the point. He used his left hand to gently push her down onto the straw. "I'm always curious about something when I meet a pretty blonde."

She smiled up at him, her teeth small and white. "Bet I know . . . what exact shade is my hair down on my valentine, right?"

Fargo nodded. "Usually it's a shade darker than the hair

on the head. But you're a pale blonde, and I'd wager it's the exact same shade."

She bit her lower lip, goading him on with her eyes. "Free peek," she said in a husky whisper. Marlene raised her hips enough to hike her dress up to her belly. Fargo gazed at a bush as fine as spun gold—a perfect match for her head.

"Free touch, too?" he asked.

"Sure, but I'll warn you—I got a short fuse. Don't start something you ain't willing to finish. I'll have me a belly ache all day."

"That won't be the part that aches," the Trailsman assured her as he unbuckled his leather gun belt. "And the part that aches will ache nice."

Fargo unfastened his buckskin trousers with one hand while the other stroked her silken bush. She spread her creamy, supple thighs wider, inviting him to feel even more. Fargo wiggled a finger into her cleft and encountered moist heat and tissue-soft folds. When he began to cosset her pliant nubbin, Marlene sighed and began to wiggle her taut, round bottom in the straw.

"Most men don't even know about *that* spot," she gasped. "Lord, Skye, you sure do."

Hey diddle-diddle and up the middle, Fargo thought as he increased the speed of his fingers, careful not to put too much pressure on her sensitive button. Marlene was cooing and moaning now, drawing her legs up and back to show him the hidden delights she had for him. By now Fargo was anvil hard and his blood throbbed in his ears. When he rose up to climb between her thighs, Marlene got a good size-up of his impressive staff and bulging sac.

"Sharlene always exaggerates," she said breathlessly. "But she was pure-dee right about you. Oh, I *will* be aching and I can't wait. Tamp me, Skye, tamp me!"

Fargo needed no orders although he always welcomed them from lust-fired women. A pulsating, tickling heat throbbed between his groin and the tip of his pizzle, demanding release. Sliding one hand under each of her satin-smooth butt cheeks, he lifted her until all he had to do was flex his hips.

Her velvet sheath opened like petals as he filled her deep,

thrust after powerful thrust probing to the deepest wet of her need. Her strong love muscle gripped and released, gripped and released him, squeezing Fargo's shaft in a hot ecstasy of pleasure. Fargo rode her so vigorously that they began to slide across the hay.

"Good god-*dang*, Skye!" she cried out. "I'm gonna pop! I'm gonnaahh, *OH*!"

She shuddered violently as a fast string of climaxes, each one more intense than the one before it, robbed her of speech. The way she kept arching her back to meet his thrusts drove Fargo to a welling pleasure that ended in volcanic release.

A few dazed minutes later Marlene stirred beside him and expelled a long sigh. "Well, now! Darlene can cuss me all she likes. I'll not cut the throat of any man who can please me like this."

"Mighty white of you," Fargo barbed as he fastened his trousers.

A sudden sneeze from behind a stack of bales made Fargo fill his hand and thumb back the hammer of his Colt. "C'mon outta there before I start tossing lead. And I better see your empty hands first."

The pale white hands were followed by a leering moon face.

"Crazy Charlie, you filthy-minded son of a bitch!" Marlene fumed. "Shoot him, Skye!"

She had forgotten to pull her dress down, and the wild-eyed lecher stared eagerly at the exposed mounds of her strawberry-tipped tits.

Charlie began capering about madly and reciting:

"Five fingers up, five fingers down,
White hairy ass goin' round and round,
Big hard prick goin' in and out,
If *that* ain't fuckin' you can throw me out!"

"Bottle it," Fargo snapped, rising to his knees and buckling on his gun belt. "And quit digging in your damn nose. I thought you were running your traps."

"Meant to." Charlie watched, grinning like a butcher's dog, as Marlene hastily covered herself. "But I snuck up to the station and heard the gals plottin' to send Marlene out here. Figured I'd see me some titties."

"You stinking goat!" Marlene snapped. "Crazy as a shite-poke and filthy-minded."

Charlie raised his voice in feminine mimic. "God-*dang*! I'm gonna pop, Skye!"

Fargo caught her wrist when Marlene grabbed for his gun. "Never mind. You needn't be in such a jo-fired hurry to kill him. Crazy or no, he's got sharp eyes and he can shoot plumb. Right now we need him. There's warpath Flatheads in this area, and the Kreeger gang could swoop down on us at any time."

Crazy Charlie tossed back his head and shrieked like a hyena. "Fargo, you talk the he-bear talk, but you sure wasn't worried about featherheads nor gangs while you was tuppin' this little hellcat blonde. 'And the part that aches will ache nice.' Hah! Does your little cunny ache nice, Marlene?"

"Why, you bald-headed baboon! You *had* teeth when you snuck up here!"

Marlene snarled like a jungle cat and leaped to her feet, but Charlie—howling like a dog in the hot moons—scrambled nimbly down the ladder. She tore after him, cussing a blue streak.

Fargo expelled a long, nasal sigh. "What in the hell," he mused aloud, "did I ever do to deserve this?"

13

Spotted Pony moved out to the very edge of a granite out-cropping high in the Bitterroot Mountains. The sun burned from a cloudless sky as pure blue as the sacred lakes of the Manitou. From here he could see as did the High Holy Ones. Water cascaded down staircase ledges, and he and Tangle Hair were so high up that a red-tailed hawk was circling below them, riding a wind current. Far below, the valleys and draws were richly timbered.

But much nearer to hand lay the new hair-face road and the strange lodge that kept white men on it. Face expression-less and unblinking, he stared at it as he spoke.

"Back east of Great Waters," he said bitterly, meaning the river whites called Missouri, "the paleface chief they call Andrew Jackson—but Sharp Knife to the red man—spoke bent words to the tribes. He told them to give up their sacred homelands and they would be given an Indian Nation. He did not tell them it would be worthless lands no white men wanted. Or that they would not rule this nation—the blue-bloused soldiers and spineless 'agents' would."

Tangle Hair nodded. "I have seen this Indian Nation. They have no horses or weapons and many starve. The land is worthless—barren plain scoured daily by fierce winds. The paleface council promises them food, but often it is not fit to eat. The meat they send is often pork that looks just like dead white men."

"I have ears for this," Spotted Pony said, still watching the station below. "And you know, shaman, that more and more of the plains warriors, too, are being forced into this 'nation.' The Arapaho were recently marched there at the point of the yellow legs' thunder sticks although they have

83

escaped—for now. Do you see this thing? Do you see that soon they will try to drive us from this land of our fathers and grandfathers?"

Tangle Hair didn't like the war chief's tone. He was hot-headed and capricious, and the medicine man felt a portent.

"Yes," he replied, "the hair-faces mean to corral all the tribes. We are in their way, and already they have begun to kill off Uncle Buffalo so that we cannot roam free. We can resist the white-eyes for only a brief time, but soon the Shining Times will be over for the red man."

These astounding words finally made Spotted Pony swivel his head to the left, staring at the older brave. "For a brief time?"

Tangle Hair nodded, pulling his red Hudson's Bay blanket tighter around his shoulders. "Yes. Only a brief time. Now there are still too few pony soldiers in our ranges to control us. And there are rumors of a great paleface war brewing beyond Great Waters. They will need their soldiers back there. But one side will win, and both sides see the red man as dogs. Soon will come the big-talking guns and many soldiers. Their magic is great and we cannot defeat them. The Shining Times are almost over."

"I see how you have become," Spotted Pony said, his voice thick with contempt. "A shaman sits in his tipi all day eating fat elk steaks cooked by the pretty squaws. He does not ride or hunt or hurl a battle lance. And soon his liver turns as white as the paleface pork."

"You would not speak this way to me in council. A shaman is responsible for seeking visions important to the tribe, for guiding his people and interpreting the signs given us by the Day Maker."

"And for turning bullets into sand?" Spotted Pony barbed.

"Yes, this also. No tribe goes into battle without counsel of the shaman."

"Is it even so?" Spotted Pony raised a hand toward the lodge below them. "You know what that place is. It keeps the white men on that big trail through our land. I am here to kill the palefaces and burn this place to the ground. I want to ride down and tell my braves we attack soon. How do you *counsel*, old man?"

"It is still too soon. I have thrown the bones." He meant the pointing bones painted with the totems of the Flathead tribe. "They pointed west, the direction of the dying sun. Only when they land pointing east can you attack."

"I have twenty braves. There are only two men down there and three squaws. Do you fear your own shadow, too?"

"I am nothing to the matter and it matters not how many living whites are down there. It is the three ghosts who still linger around the lodge. Stay away until they cross over."

During all this Spotted Pony had edged closer to Tangle Hair. Both men stood at the very precipice of the ledge.

"Perhaps," Spotted Pony said in a low, dangerous voice, "you were wrong about the bones? Perhaps they pointed east?"

Tangle Hair stubbornly shook his head. "I threw them three times. Each time was the same."

Spotted Pony nodded. "Now it is my turn to throw the bones."

He placed his hand at the small of the medicine man's back. One flex of his strong right arm sent the frail elder hurtling into space. He crashed on the pinnacles below, then rolled like so much wind-tossed dreck down a steep slope, his body causing a rock slide.

When it finally came to rest, Spotted Pony studied it until a faint smile invaded his carved-in-stone expression.

"The bones point east," he said to himself. "Soon comes the attack."

Skye Fargo, ensconced in a thicket of jack pine about a thousand yards west of Robert's Station, had been watching the Flathead braves for about five minutes. With his field glasses clearly focused on them, he could not deny what suddenly happened—nor why.

It boded ill for the defenders at Robert's Station. That older brave wearing the buffalo horns was clearly a medicine man. And the younger chief who casually pushed him to his death was almost certainly the hotheaded battle leader Spotted Pony—the eagle-tail feathers in his war bonnet trailed nearly to the ground.

Fargo knew the free-ranging tribes well enough to guess

what had happened. The medicine man, spooked by the recent burial of the Stanton brothers, had counseled against attack until those paleface spirits had crossed over to the Land of Ghosts. And Spotted Pony, little better than a renegade who rejected the law-ways and spiritual taboos of the elders, wanted to raze that station and kill the occupants.

Which meant an attack was coming soon, perhaps as early as sunrise tomorrow. And the war party, minus its shaman, would be relentless in repeating the attacks until they had achieved victory. Sieges on a forted-up position forced the defenders to expend much ammo, and Fargo knew they could not hold out long—especially with Dub Kreeger and his two surviving men also making things lively for the defenders. Fargo's plan to take the fight to the gang had ended in near disaster for him, and he hadn't yet hit upon another tactic.

With the gang on his mind, Fargo stuck to as much cover as he could find while hoofing it back to the station. By now the bloodred sun had dipped below the highest peaks of the Bitterroot Range, casting the federal road and the steep slope above it in inky shadows. Fargo was perhaps a hundred yards from the station house when a rifle spoke its piece, the sharp crack hurling in echoes from the surrounding rock faces.

Fargo felt a sharp tug at his shirt and flopped heavily to the ground.

Another shot kicked a geyser of dirt into his face, and by now Fargo realized the shots were coming from the barn.

"Charlie, you crazy son of a bitch! Stay your hand! It's Fargo coming in!"

"Sorry, boss. I couldn't see you in the twilight."

Fargo believed that and realized he should have shouted a warning when he drew into range. "My fault, old son. You damn near snuffed my wick. You're a fair hand with a rifle, all right."

Crazy Charlie came out to the corral to meet Fargo as he came in.

"I'm glad that you're keeping your eyes peeled," Fargo greeted him. "But that's two less rounds you got for your rifle. Don't be so trigger happy."

"Spot any trouble out there?"

"A heap-big ration of it." Fargo explained what he had seen up on that outcropping. "Spotted Pony doesn't strike me as a patient man," he added. "I hear he's the type who's already ten miles down the road while the rest of the tribe is discussing when to leave. Good chance they'll attack tomorrow out of the rising sun."

Charlie scratched at his wiry red hair, dug out a tick and cracked it between his teeth. "Hmm. They like to use them flaming arrows, y'know."

Fargo nodded. "I been studying on that. With new wood a fire arrow tends to go out soon after it hits. The station is new wood and wouldn't likely go up too easy. Unless they can plant fire bundles."

"What's them?"

"Bundles of rags and leaves and such tied up with buckskin thread. They use runners to stick them under the edges of buildings. Then they shoot the fire arrows into the bundles. Even then that new wood would be slow to catch fire. No, it's this barn I'm most worried about."

"Why? So far they've mostly worried about the station."

Fargo nodded. "But the Indian is a mighty notional creature. Spotted Pony has had plenty of time to con it over. He knows those horses are our only chance to light out of here. He can also see that the barn is built of shingles that will catch a spark easier than those logs of the station house. If he can burn up our mounts, or drive them out to be shot, we're gone beavers."

Charlie looked nervous in the fading light. "Overland pays fightin' wages, but I ain't looking for no Indian haircut. Well, we ain't ready to pull foot. Not less two of us ride groom's seat."

Fargo shook his head. "Riding double is all right on the flats, but not in this dangerous terrain. We'll have to dig in and hold until you break those other two draft horses to leather."

"That won't be long," Charlie promised. "I'm clemmed if I want my ball sac turned into a 'baccy pouch."

Fargo grinned. "Yeah, I see how that prospect drives you sane. Well, relax. Now that I see how you can shoot, I'm going to take over the barn and leave you up in the house with the women. The four of you should be a stout fighting force."

At this intelligence Charlie danced an excited little medicine dance. "Fargo, I'm grinnin' like a possum eating a yellow jacket! Yessir, them words is a tonic! Me, surrounded by them six tempting tits! Talk about hitching a coyote with horses."

Charlie suddenly thought of something and fell silent. "Hold on. Have you told *them* about this arrangement?"

"Nope, and they'll likely shoot me when I do. Especially after your disgusting show in the barn today—Marlene wants to cut you open from asshole to appetite."

As Fargo turned to leave, Charlie called out behind him: "When you was bulling Marlene, I seen you chewing on her tits. Do they taste like spearmint, huh? That's what I fancy they taste like."

"They taste like tits," Fargo called over his shoulder. "And if you ever spy on me again like that, I'll shoot you deader than a can of corned beef."

But Crazy Charlie was in a festive mood after Fargo's announcement. "Hey, boss?"

"Yeah?" Fargo said without turning around, still heading for the station.

"What kind of meat do you serve to Indians on their honeymoon?"

"I don't know. What kind?"

"Why, *hump* steak, of course."

Charlie's hyena-shrill laughter broke out behind Fargo. He took off his hat and shook his head with a sort of astounded resignation.

"It ain't so bad at that," he muttered. "All the Flatheads can do is kill me."

"Are you stark, staring *crazy*, Skye Fargo? No way in hell is that stinking, crazy, booger-eating fool staying up here with us! I'd sooner have the Injins in here with us—at least they wash now and then!"

Darlene was so angry that her face had turned scarlet. Fargo sat at the table eating some greasy but filling rabbit stew—Charlie had checked his snares after all.

"He won't have to stay here tonight," Fargo reasoned. "He'd just come over before sunrise. If there's no trouble by the time the sun's well up, you can send him back to the barn."

Sharlene was not so angry as her sister but wanted nothing to do with Charlie. "It don't make much sense," she objected. "We ain't had no trouble with the Indians since we buried our men. They know there's just women in the station house, and I don't think they care anymore."

Fargo wiped his mouth on his sleeve. "I told you what happened on that ledge today. If the warriors didn't care they wouldn't be hanging around here. They won't tolerate railroads or freight roads crossing their homeland, and they know that stations like this one keep the palefaces coming. I can't guarantee the attack will come tomorrow, but I'd lay high odds."

"I just bet you would," Darlene said, eyes narrowing. "You want all of us holed up in here—even Charlie—while you *claim* you'll be out in the barn."

"Where else would I be?" Fargo asked. "Philadelphia?"

"No. Packing up the gold and riding out with it."

"How can I pack up something I don't have?"

Darlene studied him with a murderous curiosity. "Because, in all that poking around and searching you been doing, you found it. And since you're not a coldblooded killer, you don't want to have to shoot us and Charlie to take it."

"What if I did find it?" Fargo shot back. "If that was the case, I'd take it back to Fort Seeley—I'm damned if I want to be a fugitive for life. And you forget that my orders are to bring you ladies back, too."

"No man," Darlene insisted, "does his duty when he has a chance to hightail it with twenty-eight thousand dollars."

"Just because you're burning up with gold fever," Fargo said, "doesn't mean every man is. I've spent my whole life out beyond the settlements, never worrying about money so long as I could buy a shot of tarantula juice now and then or a sack of oats for my horse. A few gold coins in my pocket— that's fine. A strongbox full of the stuff is just the worst kind of pox."

"Oh, that's sweet-lavender preaching, all right. No man can resist gold fever."

"Or woman," Fargo reminded her. "That's why you sent Marlene out to cut my throat today."

Now Darlene stared at her youngest sister, who sat across the trestle table from Fargo. "And a fine job she done, too. Anyhow, I didn't *tell* her to kill you. I just sorta reminded her that it's easy to kill a man while he's . . . in the throes."

"Yeah, you must think I have that gold," Fargo said. "Before you thought I had it, you were willing to let me live and provide extra firepower. Now you're afraid I'll light a shuck with it."

Darlene suddenly thought of something and hurried into the bedroom. She returned with a calfskin-bound Bible. "Take your oath on this," she demanded. "Swear your oath and I'll believe you. Say, swear to God, you don't know where that gold is."

Fargo laughed. "Why would you believe me? I wasn't Bible raised and I'm not a believer."

"That's hogwash, high pockets. A man as high-minded and preachy as you must be a believer."

Fargo shook his head in amazement. "Woman, I'm afraid your garret is unfurnished. Anyhow, I don't take oaths. Any kind. My word is my bond, and anybody who doesn't like that can kiss my ass, you included."

"See?" Darlene demanded of her sisters. "You see it with your own eyes? He won't do a simple thing like swear on the Bible. He's found where our gold is and he means to skedaddle with it, the four-flushing son of Satan."

"No need to have a hissy fit," Fargo said. "This is just gold lust twisting your brain. But if you really believe I found your hiding place, just move it again."

"Huh! If it's even there."

Fargo's face creased in a grin, flashing strong white teeth. "Go check."

Darlene's pretty face went from angry frustration to homicidal determination. Fargo had noticed that her right hand was inching closer to the huge front pocket of her calico dress. When she made the final, fast move, he filled his own gun hand quicker than thought. She gaped at the weapon that just seemed to appear in his hand like magic.

Darlene gasped. "Holy moly, Marlene! Did you see that?"

"No," Marlene replied. "I *didn't*. I must have blinked."

Fargo's tone turned hard and low. "All right, Darlene, from here on out this is the way of it. There's no more man-woman chivalry between me and you, savvy that? No pretty face, no nice tits, just a killer I mean to treat like any other man. Your sisters are still women to me so long as they don't try your gait with me. But I've had my belly full of you, and you best walk the straight and narrow with me. Now look into my eyes—*look* at me I said."

She did. Somewhat fearfully.

"Darlene, on my honor, I do *not* know where that damn gold is. I've looked but I can't find it. Do you believe me?"

"I believe you, Mr. Fargo," she replied after a few moments.

"If I do find it, I will *not* run off with it. I will return it to the U.S. Army and make sure you girls split the recovery fee. But the main mile, for me, is to get the three of you and Charlie safely out of here. Do you believe that?"

"Yes. But now *you* look at me. To hell with your recovery fee—I'm sick of the penny-ante game. It don't make a nickel's worth of difference, to me, if you run off with the gold or give it to the damn army. Either way, it's tossed down a rat hole. Our husbands was killed over that gold, and now us girls is widows with no wage earners for the rest of our lives. I don't want that gold so's we can live it up, buy fancy feathers, or gamble on the steamboats. The widows' pensions Overland pays ain't but spider leavings. We need that money to survive."

Fargo hadn't looked at it that way. He mulled her words while he tugged at his beard. "Well, that's your side of it and I take your drift. But you girls are all pretty and young, and the recovery fee will tide you until you can find new husbands. It doesn't matter what my druthers are—that payroll isn't mine to give away."

"But it's ours to take. We're not going to hand it over to you, but I promise I've had done with the plans to kill you. Do you believe that?"

Fargo studied her face for a long time. "No, not by a jugful."

Darlene's full red lips eased into a smile. "Good. Then me and you understand each other."

14

Fargo fully expected a retaliation raid from Dub Kreeger sometime after dark. It came around midnight, but instead of a mounted strike it was another intense and sustained volley of gunfire from the slope overlooking Robert's Station. He was out in the stock barn with Crazy Charlie, playing joker poker by the dim light of a covered lantern, when the first shots rent the fabric of the night.

"Here's the fandango," he announced, tossing his cards into the hay and pushing to his feet. "Remember, old son, hold off on any return fire unless they move in close enough. We need to hoard our bullets. If Spotted Pony's warriors put at us tomorrow, we'll need more than air pudding to beat them back."

He had issued the same orders to the sisters. Outside, Dub Kreeger, Link Jeffries, and Willy Hanchon made the air fairly hum as they emptied their carbines as quickly as they could reload and lever rounds. Bullets thwacked into the sturdy station house with a sound like hail pelting it. Fargo knew those rounds weren't penetrating the thick logs and reinforced door, but the thin-shingled barn was a softer target.

He and Charlie hunched behind bales of hay as rounds punched through the walls and hummed past them with a blowfly drone, some striking sparks when they hit horseshoes or tools. They had already moved the horses into the last stalls, but the animals nickered and kicked at the walls in fright—all except the bullet-savvy Ovaro. Fargo grinned when he spotted the stallion calmly munching hay.

"God's trousers!" Crazy Charlie exclaimed when a bullet spun his hat sideways. "Them motherlovin' bastards must've struck a lode of bullets. They ain't let up for two minutes."

"Jasper told me they hit the armory right after they busted

92

out of the stockade," Fargo replied. "The Spencer is a good gun, but at the rate they're burning powder there's a good chance they'll crack their firing pins. Those carbines aren't meant for sustained fire at this clip."

Fargo listened carefully to make sure the trio wasn't moving in closer. So far the three women had shown good discipline, not returning a shot. Suddenly the firing ceased.

"Hey, Marlene!" bellowed a voice Fargo recognized as Kreeger's. "How's come you and your sisters been giving that velvet twixt your legs to a saddle bum like Fargo, hanh? That lanky crusader won't share them yaller boys with you—he's just a jackleg law dog! I know all about that army lickspittle—he means to return that payroll to the goddamn gum'ment!"

Again the firing erupted for a full minute, deadly hailstones that raised swirls of dust in the barn.

"Hey, Marlene! I've had a case on you ever since I first seen you bathing in that pool! Throw in with me and we'll *all* be living high on the hog! I know how to treat a beautiful woman."

"Yeah," Marlene's voice fired back. "Just like you treated my husband."

"Well, now, actually I killed the other two. It was Willy here what done for your man."

"'At's right!" a second voice rang out of the night. "I put the gun barrel about six inches behind his curly head and blowed them brain curdles right out his skull. He flopped over dead and his pants filled up with shit."

"But you tricky bitches got that gold," Dub Kreeger went on. "Ain't no swinging dick in the world gonna come up here and save your lily-white ass. I done killed that army officer, and Fargo ain't man enough to save the three of you by hisself. Ain't that the straight, Fargo?"

It grew so silent there was no sound except the wind whining through the passes.

"S'matter, Fargo? You gotcher dick in one a them bitches, or you just yellow? C'mon outside, Trailsman, and settle our hash for us."

In truth, Fargo had gone outside when all this jaw-jacking had begun. Holding his Henry at a high port, sticking to the generous shadows made by a cloud-covered moon, he advanced

93

down the road until his battle-honed ears told him the men were right above him. He moved into the rocks and crouched, waiting for what would come.

"We gave you a chance!" Kreeger shouted. "Now chew on lead!"

Again the outlaw trio opened fire, and Fargo immediately spotted the yellow-orange spear tips of muzzle flash. It was going to be a tough shot—he couldn't see any of the men nor even a silhouette against the bleak sky.

He picked the man in the middle, swung the Henry up into his shoulder socket, and aimed just above the muzzle flash. He had levered a round into the chamber before he left the barn, and now he followed the BRASS formula that had kept him alive in a land where the first shot is often the only shot: Breathe . . . Relax . . . Aim . . . Take up the Slack . . . Squeeze the trigger.

The Henry bucked into his shoulder. A scream so high-pitched it tingled Fargo's scalp brought the firing above him to an immediate halt.

"My eye!" shrieked the unrecognizable voice. "Oh, Christ, Dub, I'm shot in the goddamn eye!"

"Let's dust, Willy!" Kreeger's urgent voice ordered. "Fargo's out there close!"

"My eye!" the voice that had to be Link Jeffries roared. "Dub, don't leave—"

A short gun barked and the voice fell silent. Fargo grinned. If a man wounded in the shoulder was too much baggage, one plugged in the eye was a ball and chain.

The retreating men were invisible on the dark slope, and though Fargo could have shot at their noise, it seemed foolish to provide muzzle flash for them to deal him the same misery he had just dealt Jeffries.

All of this had been overheard from the station. "Skye?" Marlene's worried voice called out. "Skye, you out there?"

Fargo ignored her, not about to give up his position. He heard the two men scrabbling on the loose slope, then the sound of horses heading upslope.

"I'm still in one piece," he called back toward the station. "Give me a minute."

Fargo picked his way up to their firing position and

couldn't miss Link Jeffries. The huge man lay dead on his back, his face a bloody death mask. His companions had enough presence of mind to grab his carbine, but not his Colt Navy .38 and his nearly full shell belt. Fargo had to strain mightily to remove it from under the heavy corpse.

It was Darlene who let him in at the station. Her eyes lit up at the sight of the gun and ammo. "Praise the Lord! You killed another one. That's two cockroaches down. Which one this time?"

"Link Jeffries."

"He was the big one," Sharlene chimed in. "Too bad it wasn't Dub or that rat-face son of a bitch Willy Hanchon. It was them two killed our men."

"You *still* think Skye is a fraidycat?" Marlene demanded of her sister.

"T'hell with that schoolgirl crap," Fargo cut in. "If I'm right, this set-to tonight is a fart in a hurricane compared to what's coming tomorrow. Remember what I told you girls. Fill up the washtub so I can drag it in here. Be ready to put out any fires before they can spread. Don't stare out those loopholes too long at one time—a Flathead can thread an arrow through the eye of a needle. Don't waste ammo, but if you see a good shot, take it. Indians don't fight to the last man—if we kill one or two, they might withdraw."

"They won't attack," Darlene said with conviction. "They know our men are gone."

Fargo stopped in front of the door and turned back to look at her. "Put that foolish notion away from your mind. These red sons are wrathy. This new road was built right over an Indian trace stretching back a hundred years. And now white squatters are taking over their territory. They soured on the white man a long time ago, Darlene, and the white *woman* won't stop them. I recommend you and your sisters do what I say, and make sure you're all up and on the line before sunrise."

"I will," Marlene said solemnly.

"Me, too," Sharlene pitched in.

"I will, too," Darlene added, "just to humor all of you."

Fargo joined Crazy Charlie in the stock barn and began an all-night vigil from the loft doors.

"Why watch for John after dark?" Charlie asked. "Everybody knows Injins don't attack at night."

"Don't *usually* attack at night," Fargo corrected him. "Like I said, the red man is notional. Don't forget, Spotted Pony murdered his own medicine man right before my eyes. If he believed the law-ways he wouldn't have the stones to do that—it would leave him wandering in the Forest of Tears, alone and blind, for eternity."

"Sounds like that jasper is as loco as I am."

Fargo shifted his eyes from the shadow-mottled road out front to Crazy Charlie. "As loco as you *seem.* Anyhow, I'm not too worried they'll actually attack before sunrise. But I'd bet a dollar to a doughnut they send a runner on foot to plant fire bundles around that station—and likely the barn."

"I can't see why you made me douse the lantern," Charlie carped. "Hell, it's darker than the inside of a boot in here."

"That's the point, chowderhead. It's a dark night out there. If we're going to spot any featherheads sneaking up with fire bundles, we'll have to get our eyes adjusted to total darkness."

"I spoze them kind of tricks are what you rugged scouts count on. Me, I'm a coward and I prefer to dupe my way out of danger. The first time these red arabs swooped down on us, I stripped naked, scooped up a dead barn snake, and ran out among 'em doing a jig and singing verses from 'Lu-lu Girl.' Them untutored bachelors of the forest took off like scalded dogs."

Fargo grinned. "Mighty quick thinking for a crazy man. Trouble is, with a renegade killer like Spotted Pony you can't go to that well twice. You got any more big ideas in that line?"

"The well is dry, boss. If I pull that again, I'll end up looking like a pincushion. It's dead palefaces seem to spook them the most."

Something suddenly clicked in Fargo's mind. "Fargo," he muttered, "what is wrong with you and what doctor told you so?"

"Christ," Charlie said, "you've got too close to me and gone crazy yourself. What are you mumbling?"

"Never mind. Can you fashion a pointed stake and pound it into the ground in front of the station house? A strong one about five feet long?"

"Easier than rolling off a log. But what's the play?"

Fargo stood up. "I'll tell you later. Right now I have to go retrieve our guest from that slope. And it's going to be like moving a mountain from a mountain. Get thrashing on that stake and keep your eyes skinned for trouble."

Fargo felt his way to the ladder, climbed down to the ground, and slipped outside with his Henry dangling from his left hand. He paused for a minute to look and listen, then took a good whiff of the breeze: most Western tribes used plenty of rancid bear grease to hold their hair, and a trained nose could sometimes detect it. Then he led the Ovaro from its stall and stood beside it in the corral, watching its sensitive ears and nose. But the vigilant stallion failed to alert.

Fargo stalled him again and headed down the dark federal road, turning left at the spot where he had shot Link Jeffries. He scrambled up the slope, gripped the huge corpse under the arms, and grunted at the effort of getting the body into motion. At least the slope was on his side until he reached the level expanse of the road. He paused again to listen, then began the arduous task of dragging the cumbersome body back to the station. Despite the high-altitude chill of the stiff breeze, Fargo was sweating copiously by the time he made it back.

Crazy Charlie was waiting for him, the stake ready. "I figured out what you had in mind," he greeted the Trailsman. "Think it'll work?"

"Not if we just leave him here and give them time to get used to it." Fargo replied between panting breaths. "We'll have to spring it on them. Look, he's got a rope belt. I'm gonna hold the big son of a bitch up while you lash him to the stake under his arms. You'll have to use a double hitch to hold him."

It was a struggle and twice the body slumped to the ground. Finally, however, Link Jeffries was propped up. Fargo used a strip of rawhide from his possibles bag to tie the head up separately.

"Ladies," he called through the door, "can you hear me? It's Fargo. Snuff the light before you open the door."

A few moments later the door swung open and the two men stepped inside.

"I smell that crazy baboon!" Darlene's angry voice rang out of the darkness. "Fargo, you said Charlie wasn't coming over here until sunrise! His very name is gall and worm-wood to me."

Marlene's voice chimed in. "Skye, get him outta here before I shoot him! That scurvy-ridden whoreson spied on us today, the filthy slug!"

"Come down off your hind legs, girls," Fargo replied, biting his lower lip to keep from laughing. "He's not here to camp. I just need to borrow a sheet. And some twine or strong string if you got it."

A candle flared to life on the trestle table, throwing a weak yellow-orange glow around the big room.

"A sheet?" Darlene demanded. "Don't tell me you've dug up another woman? Didn't Marlene wear it out for you?"

"The ass waggeth its ears," Fargo said calmly. "I need the sheet to help fight off the Indians."

Darlene snorted. "So you're still pushing that Indian attack line? I'm telling you we're safe from them."

"They've greased their faces and struck the war trail," Fargo told her. "Nobody's safe."

"Hunh! I prefer to credit my own eyes," Darlene insisted. "I ain't seen nothing for days."

"The sign is there, all right. Too many owl hoots lately in a place too high for owls. Trouble is only a fox-step away."

"Fargo," Charlie butted in, "is a famous Indian fighter. I think he knows more about red John than a slut from Pennsylvania does."

"Why, you mouthy varmint! I'll kill you where you stand!"

"Don't touch that repeater," Fargo warned as she lunged toward the gun belts hanging on the wall. "If you're gonna kill him, use a shovel. We need every bullet."

"You girls show me some titties," Charlie said in a hopeful voice, "and I'll shut pan."

"You seen plenty today, you ugly toad," Marlene snapped. "I ain't never showing you mine again."

"I always get the little end of the horn," Charlie whined to Fargo. "I have a mind to let these three witches fend for themselves."

"Never mind all this catarumpus," Fargo said to the room in general. "Charlie, just caulk up. Marlene, get me that sheet and string, wouldja?"

Marlene ducked into the bedroom. Darlene stood with arms akimbo, staring at Fargo. "Well, you've had both my sisters. Which one was best?"

Fargo lifted a shoulder. "I never could tell the difference between two beautiful roses."

Darlene snorted. "Stuff! You're only saying that because Sharlene is here. I reckon you figure I'm next?"

"With me, it's always the lady's choice."

"Well don't count on that. They'll announce holidays in hell before I ever give it up to you."

"As for me," Charlie piped up, "I druther stick my face in a sheepherder's ass than stick my pizzle in you."

"No, you spawn of dung beetles, you'd rather stick your face in the *sheep's* ass!"

"All right," Fargo intervened, "both of you bottle it. A bunch of damn stable sergeants don't talk like this."

"Here you go, Skye," Marlene said, emerging with a bunched-up sheet. "Is fishing line all right?"

"It'll do, cupcake."

"What's it for?" Sharlene asked as Fargo turned toward the door.

"A little surprise for our riled-up Flatheads. Girls, I'm going to attach this line through the sheet, then feed it through one of the loopholes. Sometime after sunrise you'll hear me raise a shout to let 'er rip. That's your signal to tug the line inside."

"Why?" Darlene demanded. "There's not going to be an Indian attack tomorrow. With our men gone, us girls is just chicken-fixin's to the savages."

"Tomorrow before the mist burns off, lady. There's bad trouble on the spit, and lollygaggers will die hard."

The fat stub of tallow candle burning on the table suddenly flickered as if to emphasize Fargo's prediction.

Darlene was unfazed. "Cowplop! You're just trying to scare us so we'll stay holed up while you—"

"Have it your own way," Fargo cut her off. "I hope you're right about the attack. But I haven't stayed above the ground all these years by hoping. I say there's one helluva dustup coming, and I mean a humdinger."

15

When the two men were halfway back to the barn, Fargo stopped Charlie with a hand on his arm.

"Stay up in the loft," Fargo told him, "but get some sleep. I'm going to be on roving patrol out here. I'll roust you out when it's time for you to join the women."

"Ahuh. But say, Fargo, what's biting at that damn Darlene? The other two girls believe you about the Indian raid, but she's dead set against the notion."

"That's gold fever riding herd on her brain, Charlie. It works on a woman just like on a man. Right now her brain is a one-trick pony, and getting that gold down from these mountains is the only trick she cares about. She claims to believe me when I say I don't plan to steal it, but she knows I plan to return it to the army, and that's as good as stealing it, to her."

"Ever since I hired on here, I been noticing how it was her, not her husband Cort, who run the whole shebang around here. I knew women like her back in Arkansas— acted like they owned every raccoon that crapped on their back forty."

Fargo took a slow glance around. The clouds had blown off and silver-white moonlight limned everything in a ghostly aura.

"Think the *peaux-rouges* are close by?" Charlie asked, his voice tight with nervousness.

"Seems likely. They'd want to be in position for a sunrise strike."

The Ovaro suddenly nickered from inside the barn, and Fargo felt a stirring of belly flies. Telling Charlie to hold back, he scurried toward the looming dark shape of the barn.

He propped his Henry up outside the door and shucked his Colt out of the holster, thumb-cocking the weapon and slipping into the dark interior. For a minute Fargo just listened, hearing little besides the snuffling of horses. Then, sticking to the shadows along the long east wall, he crept farther inside on cat feet.

The Ovaro nickered again, and Jasper Dundee's cavalry sorrel picked it up. There was definitely an intruder, Fargo realized—and a good chance it was a Flathead brave getting set to torch the place.

Fargo would have vastly preferred a white intruder. A well-trained Indian warrior knew fifty ways to kill a man before breakfast, all of them equally unpleasant. And they were pitiless in their resolve: sometimes the old battle chiefs would even torture a captured baby and make the young warriors watch just to harden their bark.

All this looped through Fargo's mind as he advanced farther into the barn. Suddenly pandemonium broke out. The Ovaro gave a high-pitched whicker of anger and Fargo heard several powerful kicks, followed by a fierce snarling that he recognized instantly. He raced headlong for the last stall, expecting the worst.

Instead, when he thumb-scratched a lucifer into flame he found a dead badger lying at the stallion's feet, its neck broken from a kick.

Grinning, the Trailsman scratched the Ovaro's withers fondly. "Well, old campaigner, it was fight or show yellow, huh? That's one barnyard raider who won't come sassy again."

The Ovaro twisted his head around and nosed Fargo's chest in greeting.

"I know you want to run the stall kinks out. I'm tired of hoofing it everywhere, too. But right now we have to hold back, y'unnerstan'? We'll soon hit the trail again."

Fargo leathered his shooter and went back outside.

"What was all that ruckus?" Crazy Charlie demanded. "Did you put an Indian with his ancestors?"

"Not hardly. My horse put a badger with his."

"A badg—now, Fargo, I admit that stallion of yours is one for sheer, spiteful cussedness when he's pushed. I pulled his oats too quick and he bit me a good one on the ampersand. But horses don't kill badgers."

"Tell that to the dead badger in his stall. By the way, toss it when you go inside. And be careful: I didn't toss a finishing shot into it."

"It's just I never—"

"Never mind all that," Fargo cut him off impatiently. "Have you still got those two blasting cans I gave you?"

"Up in the loft."

"All right, for now we'll just leave 'em there. We're gonna need all our ammo, so remember—no shooting at shadows. But we can't use those powder cans up too fast, neither. If this Spotted Pony is as reckless as I hear, we'll prob'ly need to send quite a few of his braves to hunt for the White Buffalo before we're out of this. But there'll likely be more than one attack, so let's see how our little surprise under the sheet does at unstringing their nerves."

A match flared to life and Crazy Charlie leaned into the flame, lighting a cheap Mexican cigar Fargo had given him yesterday.

"Chuck that butt, you damn fool," Fargo snapped, slapping it out of his mouth. "Nothing like lighting the target for 'em. Maybe you are crazy."

Charlie began capering in a Virginia reel.

"My brain is soft, my pecker too,
And titties make me swoon,
I like to crap inside a shoe,
And piss beneath the moon."

"Get back to the barn," Fargo ordered, his face wrinkling in disgust as if he'd just whiffed skunk.

"I just made that up," Charlie boasted.

Fargo's voice lowered an octave. "Are you bolted to the ground? I said get back to the barn. And give over with this soft-brain nonsense or these sunburned warriors will use your teeth for dice."

As Charlie Waites, alias Crazy Charlie, scampered toward the barn, Fargo stood in numb confusion, unable to believe the mare's nest he had ridden into. He was on the verge of wringing his hands like a helpless midwife. The Trailsman was no stranger to rough scrapes, but this one wasn't just rough—it was insane. Instead of a seasoned Indian fighter like Jasper Dundee to side him, he had three beautiful women of dubious loyalty and a fool who couldn't put on his own socks.

One consolation, he thought in a burst of black humor—he wasn't likely to end up buzzard bait. After all, there were no buzzards up this high. He headed toward the road.

"'I like to crap inside a shoe,'" he repeated Charlie's verse, shaking his head. "I'll have to keep my boots away from that moonstruck simpleton."

As the moon climbed toward its zenith and the thin mountain air developed a knife edge of chill, Fargo stayed in almost constant motion. Hugging shadows, moving in a low crouch, he traveled from barn to station house and back, always on the watch for Indians planting fire bundles. He had left his Henry in the stock barn to free his hands for a knife fight—experience had taught him that sudden encounters with red warriors often became blade contests before a man could draw and cock a handgun.

He did not intend to reveal himself, however, and would fight only if he was discovered. Although he watched that northern slope like a cat on a rat, he had little hope of spotting an intruder. The free-ranging tribes were masters of cover and concealment, and by the time you spotted them it was usually too late.

Fargo had just circled the barn when Charlie's raucous shout made him flinch. "Hey, Fargo, you out there? Care for a snort? I got some potato whiskey that would raise blood blisters on new leather."

"Well, I'm a Dutchman," Fargo muttered, face flushing with the warmth of sudden anger. "I'll baste his bacon good."

He ducked into the barn and felt for the ladder, climbing it into the loft. Charlie, following orders, sat in the loft door. Although a jug sat beside him, Fargo did not smell the usual odors of a drunken revelry.

"Are you corned?" he demanded.

"Not so's you'd notice," Charlie replied. "Just a nip now

and again to keep warm. Thought you might like a bracer, too."

Fargo's anger receded. "Well I'm sorry to spoil your big time, Charlie, but you can't be bellowing like that. We want the featherheads to think we're sleeping."

"Well, God kiss me if I see the sense of that. If me hollering will keep them off, won't that keep them fire bundles away too?"

"We want the fire bundles planted."

"God-in-whirlwinds, Fargo, whose colors are you flying?"

"Hush down, chucklehead. As soon as the runner leaves, I soak all the bundles in water and put them back. That way they fail to ignite during the attack. And that's why I don't want to kill the runner—so Spotted Pony believes everything is hunky-dory. Now, is that jake by you, John-a-dreams?"

"Sure, boss, sure. But if you *want* them bundles put down, why not just lay low?"

"Because I can't be certain the runner won't fire them up tonight instead of waiting for an attack tomorrow. And this barn would go up just like"—Fargo snapped his fingers—"*that*. When horses panic in a fire, it's the devil's own work to lead them to safety."

Crazy Charlie shook his head in the silvery moonlight. "I thought I was a Westerner by now. But I'm still just one a them soft-handed town bastards from back east. I'd starve and go naked if I had to live like you."

"Well, I believe you've seen the elephant a few times," Fargo said absently, gazing out the loft door. From the position of the polestar he guessed it was perhaps three hours until dawn. "And none of us is eating hot eggs and scrapple. But this fight I think is coming at sunrise ain't about you winning laurels. If those sash-warriors manage to catch us flat-footed, we're under. Savvy that?"

"Sure, but say, why do they call them sash—"

"You flap your mouth too damn much. Just sew up your lips and catch some sleep. I'll roust you out when it's time to head over to the station."

Fargo made his way to the ladder, climbed down, and headed for the faint square of light where one barn door stood open. But the moment he stepped outside if felt like a boulder had crashed into him.

Fargo flew sideways off his feet and hit the ground hard, his attacker clinging to him like a tight noose. Fargo smelled rancid bear grease and knew he was up against it. He spotted the brave holding him down, his right hand poised to plunge the obsidian knife. Fargo could reach neither his own knife nor gun, but experience in ground-fighting tactics made him react without delay.

He brought his right thumb hard into the brave's left eye, eliciting a grunt of pain. Before the warrior could recover Fargo threw a short punch into his throat, knocking the breath from his attacker. The Trailsman took advantage of these twin blows and got his knees against the Flathead's chest, hurling him clear and shooting to his feet.

Fargo slapped his holster and found it empty—his Colt had been thrown clear when he flew to the ground. However, there was no time to look for it—the brave had recovered and was back on his feet, rushing Fargo.

Fargo snatched the Arkansas toothpick from his boot and squared off to meet the attack. He had learned over the years that Indians used their blades differently from whites. Whereas white men usually lunged in for a deep thrust into vitals, Indians preferred a fast, furious slashing attack, cutting their opponent to ribbons and bleeding the fight out of them.

That's exactly what this one had in mind now. He danced left and right, slashing rapidly with his knife as he edged in closer, trying to unnerve this buckskin-clad white man. At one point he surprised Fargo by leaping forward enough to slash Fargo's chest. Luckily, the thick buckskin shirt took most of it and Fargo felt only a brief lick of hot pain.

Fargo feinted left, then spun around rapidly on one heel and slashed the brave's left shoulder deep. He grunted again. Fargo had no intention of making this a prolonged waltz. He suddenly dropped onto his ass and put his long legs to good use, wrapping them around the Indian's knees and rolling over hard to bring him down. In an eyeblink Fargo was on him, driving the toothpick deep into his abdomen—so deep that Fargo felt the rush of heat on his hand as the brave's vitality escaped.

He sat there a few moments, breathing raggedly. He sleeved sweat off his forehead, wiped his blade on the Flathead's legging and then untangled himself from the corpse and retrieved his Colt. Now he spotted the fire bundle the brave had been stuffing under the barn. Several more sat near it in a fiber sack.

"Shit, piss, and corruption," he swore quietly, his voice a razor-thin whisper. When this brave didn't return, Spotted Pony would know the bundles weren't in place. Nor would he trust any that were.

"There's a hoodoo on me," he speculated quietly.

But he realized that logic was hind side foremost—the hoodoo was on this place, not him. That new road reflecting like a white ribbon in the moonlight—he had ridden this way when it was barely a mountain-goat trail used by a few hearty fur trappers. Criminals like Dub Kreeger couldn't use this high lonesome for a haven without that damnable road, and the onward rush of civilization would not be squeezing out the horse tribes and goading them to war.

Fargo glanced at the corpse, still spuming blood. He took no pleasure in the kill. In some ways he and that dead warrior were kindred spirits being hunted down by railroad tycoons, miners, and land speculators.

"Charlie," he called out. "You still awake?"

"Sure, boss. What's on the spit?"

"Can you make another stake just like the last one?"

"Would a cow lick Lot's wife? What's it for?"

"You'll see when you come outside. C'mon over to the station and get me when you're done."

"Christ, Fargo, who did you kill? Was it that bitch Darlene? Didja—"

"Just hold your powder, mooncalf, and get on that job. Mighty damn quick we're gonna have warpath Indians looking to take our topknots."

16

Fargo knocked on the station door and called out his name. Only the tallow candle burned within, but it was enough to show him Marlene's ashen face as she opened the door. Sharlene sat at the table using a tin can to cut biscuit rounds.

"Where's Darlene?" he asked. "Counting her gold?"

"She went to bed," Marlene replied. "Said she wasn't gonna miss no sleep over some fool notion like an Indian attack."

"But we believe it's coming," Sharlene piped up. "And even if it ain't, Dub Kreeger is still out there somewheres and that rat-face Willy Hanchon with him."

"Oh, the red peril has already opened the ball," Fargo assured the sisters. "Darlene is welcome to go visit the Flathead corpse in front of the barn. She won't find him too talkative, though."

"We're under attack?" Marlene cried.

"Calm down, sugar britches, so far there's only been one. He ripped open my shirt, damn his bones, but he's in the Happy Hunting Grounds now."

Fargo explained about the fire bundles. "I had to kill him or he'd a cut me to trap bait, but it's a bad piece of luck. Now Spotted Pony's band will plant bundles during the attack. I see you've got the tub of water ready. Keep a close eye on the base of the walls."

"Skye, did you just leave the Injin's corpse out there?" Sharlene asked.

"Honey, I'll be earmarked and hog-tied before I bury any man that tries to douse my light. I've got a better use for him."

Even as Fargo said this, muffled pounding noises sounded out front.

"Is that Charlie?" Marlene asked, wringing her hands nervously.

Fargo nodded, a faint shadow of a smile touching his lips. "We're going to mount this dead Flathead right next to Link Jeffries. Link is a bull, but the brave is skinny, so I figure the sheet will cover both of them."

Sharlene stood up, one floury hand going to her throat. "Skye Fargo, do you mean to say there's a body under that sheet you borrowed?"

Fargo grinned. "What, did you think it was a sculpted masterpiece I was going to unveil for the Indians?"

Marlene giggled. "I think it's funny."

After a moment Sharlene relented. "It is," she agreed and both women giggled like schoolgirls.

"The hell's all the ruckus in there?" Darlene's voice complained from the bedroom.

"Why don't you roll out and knock us up some grub pronto?" Fargo called out. "You're paring the cheese mighty close to the rind, girl. These noble savages attack early and they can hang on like ticks. Won't be any chance to eat once you hear the war whoop."

"Fargo, you don't know 'B' from a bull's foot. It's none of your dicker how late I sleep, and anyhow, there ain't no Injin attack coming."

"Sis, you're full of sheep dip," Marlene said. "You could train mules to be stubborn."

Fargo gave up and lifted the rawhide thong that served as a latchstring. "How's it going out here, Charlie?"

"Thissen was light, boss. I drug him over and got him all trussed up. Don't seem like so much now, hey? He's spread his last brag 'bout how he's gonna paint the landscape red with paleface blood."

"Just mind your pints and quarts," Fargo warned, studying the grisly sight in the buttery moon wash. "This fellow damn near sent me under, and there's more like him coming."

"Ahuh. Just touching him fair gave me the fidgets," Charlie admitted.

"I see you've got your rifle, so just toss the sheet over him and then go on inside. I'll head over to the barn. And damn it, Charlie, *don't* go carrying on about their damn tits. A

108

man's got to match his gait to the horse he's riding, and right now you're riding a man killer. Marlene's ready to whip your hide six ways to Sunday, and we can't afford to lose a fighter."

Crazy Charlie tossed his head back and howled. "Sneaky Pete from Silver Street, with sixteen inches of dangling meat."

"You hairy-headed chicken plucker," Fargo said, but without any real venom. As Charlie headed toward the door of the station, Fargo detained him with a hand on his arm. "Look, we could all be killed here today. Why'n't you satisfy my curiosity and tell me where that gold is?"

Charlie paused dramatically, then said in a voice just above a whisper, "'Tis a long lane that has no turning, boss."

"What, is that some kind of clue?"

"Nope. Just an old saying my mother liked."

Fargo doubled up his fist and Charlie scampered toward the door.

As Fargo expected, the Flatheads attacked out of the rising sun, their shrill yipping unnerving after the quiet of the mountain night. Somewhere they had laid hands on an army bugle and one of the braves added to the raucous din. Others blew ear-piercing notes on eagle-bone whistles. The Trailsman had been caught up in many such clamorous Indian charges, yet they always made his stomach fist in nervous fear.

From past experience they knew the loft door was trouble, and Fargo barely tugged his face aside before a flurry of deadly arrows *fwipped* past him. The Flatheads made particularly dangerous arrow points from flaked flint—they tore a destructive path entering the body and were nearly impossible to extract. They were often also smeared with animal dropping, and Fargo knew even a minor wound would prove lethal.

Half the warriors peeled off to attack the station house while the rest, as Fargo had anticipated, headed for the stock barn. He raced to the far side of the loft where he could see the wide door below that opened onto the corral. He had one blasting can left and took it from his possibles bag. The moment the door edged open, he scratched a lucifer, lit the fuse, and flipped the can underhand so that it hit the door and bounced outside.

The explosion rocked the stock barn and momentarily silenced the din without. Seizing the moment Fargo half climbed, half leaped down the ladder and waded into the acrid black smoke at the front of the barn.

One brave lay dead just outside the barn while others were escaping the big-medicine blast. Shooting from the hip, Fargo dropped two ponies. For the moment, at least, the Flathead warriors wanted nothing to do with the barn although some launched flaming arrows into the old wood. The Henry bucked over and over as Fargo targeted these warriors, dropping ponies—an Indian was loathe to fight afoot and had to be taken up by another mounted warrior. This seriously curtailed their fighting ability.

The station, however, was up against it and the battle was in full pitch. Fargo spotted the war leader spurring his men to reckless deeds. Spotted Pony sent braves in close to plant fire bundles, but the defenders inside had already wounded two. Nonetheless, Fargo noted gratefully that Charlie and the girls were being sparing with their ammo.

Still shrouded in smoke, Fargo dropped to one knee, tossed the long Henry into his shoulder, and dropped a bead on the war chief. Before he could squeeze off a round, however, the fletching of an arrow razor-burned his cheek. Fargo was forced to pivot left and sight on a warrior charging him with reckless abandon, eager for the glory of a coup. Fargo's next shot wiped him from his buffalo-hide saddle.

By now Fargo had lost sight of Spotted Pony in the wheeling confusion around the station. He settled for well-aimed shots to stop braves trying to plant fire bundles. Nonetheless, at least one small fire was burning, and Fargo hoped that water from inside could stem the flames.

Fargo dropped two more braves, but it was clear that Spotted Pony—a man willing to kill his own shaman—was not worried about losing face if he sacrificed too many warriors. With shrill cries he egged his men on even as more realized the hair-face near the barn was their biggest problem.

Hard-hitting arrows quilled the damaged door behind

Fargo, some hissing past so close that he felt the wind-rip. Seeing a second fire licking at one corner of the station, Fargo dropped to a prone position and bellowed above the din, "NOW, CHARLIE!"

He crossed his fingers and watched the sheet slide back from the two corpses. At first there was little reaction. Caught up in the heat of the attack, only a few braves even noticed the abominable sight of their dead comrade next to a giant paleface. But as more noticed, the racket diminished. A few Flatheads, perhaps the most superstitious, fled east down the white man's road in full rout.

The rest, however, merely withdrew and milled in confusion as Spotted Pony, apparently unfazed, tried to rally them to the fight. Fargo rose to a kneeling offhand position, placed his notch on the renegade's head, and squeezed off a round. Spotted Pony's skull shattered in a spray of blood and brain curdles, and he slid off his pony like a sack of grain.

That tore it, Fargo realized with a heavy sigh of relief. With the head of the snake cut off, and his braves already nerve-rattled, the braves disappeared in a boiling cloud of dust. Nor were they likely to return anytime soon once the tribal elders realized how many had been sent under by the reckless Spotted Pony.

"God dawg!" Charlie greeted him when he opened the door for Fargo. "I figured all of us for gone coons. Them gut-eaters never pitched into the game like *this* before."

"Everybody all right?" Fargo asked, glancing around at the three women.

"They got a couple fires going," Marlene replied, her face still ashen. "But we soaked 'em good from inside."

"Go ahead," Darlene said aggressively, "tell me how I gotta swallow back my words about the Indian attack."

Fargo, his face powder-blackened, took her measure with his shrewd, sun-crinkled eyes. She was hardly dressed to repel an Indian attack. She wore a straw hat trimmed with blue ribbons and an ostrich feather. In her embarrassment, her delicately carved cheeks glowed like Roman beauties.

"We've already skinned that grizz," Fargo told her. "Me and you got new battles ahead, anh?"

Fargo turned to Charlie, who was digging in his nose

111

with an exploratory finger. "You, John-a-dreams. Let's get outside and haul those bodies away from the station. We'll use my stallion to drag the dead ponies away."

"We could keep one of the ponies to eat," Charlie suggested. "Horse meat is good fixin's. But butchering ain't my line."

Fargo nodded. "All your notions aren't crazy, are they? Just rough-gut it for a few steaks—we ain't putting down roots in this place."

"I see you're in charge now," Darlene interjected.

Fargo's teeth flashed at her through his beard. "Why, I've been in charge since I got here, sugarplum."

"This is Overland property, not the army's. It ain't none of your picnic."

"He's in charge of *me*," Marlene said spitefully, handing Fargo a cold biscuit and a dipper of water.

"Me, too," Sharlene chimed in. "Darlene figures there ain't room but for one big frog in the puddle, and that big frog is her."

"Of course you two would lick his . . . boots," Darlene said. "He's put your ankles behind your ears and you want more of it. But Mr. Fargo will see the sun rise in the west before he ever gets my best."

At this, Charlie broke into a fast jig. "Man proposes, but God disposes. Gals, I fought like a wildcat. Show me some titty."

Three weapons were suddenly trained on him, and Fargo barely managed to drag Charlie outside in time to spare him from a new air shaft.

17

"Son of a beer-bellied bitch! Didja *see* that, Dub?" exclaimed Willy Hanchon. "Brother, I never seen the like."

Dub Kreeger's predatory pale ice eyes were still aimed at Robert's Station well below them. The two men were ensconced in a nest of boulders so high up the mountain slope that cottony wisps of cloud surrounded them.

"Hell, yes, I saw it," he snarled in reply. "I been right here next to you."

Willy's furtive face twisted into a nervous frown. "That goddamn Fargo wasn't born in the woods to be scared by an owl. I counted damn near twenty braves, and he sent them running faster than a river when the snow melts."

"He knows shit from apple butter," Dub conceded. "He's been wandering the frontier prac'ly from when he was a stripling. I told you he had sap in him."

Willy pulled at his beard-stubbed chin. "He's killed Fats and Link. Could be that's fair warning to us."

"Willy, you're a good man in a set-to, but you always was a calamity-howler. Never mind the damn 'legend' of Skye Fargo. Crockett was a legend, too, but he got cut down like a pig. If greasers can put the lie to a legend, so can we."

"Dub, one reason I took French leave from the army was on account I don't want to stick my neck out. Taking on Fargo is more risk than fightin' savages."

"You dumb galoot! Willing to wound but afraid to strike. You got one lousy dollar a day for fighting red John. Right now we're talking twenty-eight thousand dollars—that's fourteen thousand simoleons apiece. Ain't *that* worth sticking your neck out?"

Willy blinked his tiny eyes rapidly, mulling it. "It's a

powerful lot of money, sure enough. It could last me the rest of my days."

"Why, you'd live like King Shit! Top-shelf liquor, top-shelf whores—you could live in a fancy hotel with one a them velvet ropes you pull to send a boy running. Mister, you'd be *some*."

Willy thought about all this and slowly nodded. "Yeah, it'd be great larks, huh? But I ain't too damn keen to take on Fargo."

"Who is? We don't need to call him out. We just need to kill him."

"Sure, but they need ice water in hell, too. *How* do we kill him? That bastard is tougher than a two-bit steak."

Dub's thin lips curled back off his teeth—his version of a smile. "How? For one thing, we change our tactics. So far we just been raiding on the station trying to get them to burn their ammo. You seen today how they held back with their barking irons—they've twigged our game. From here on out we got only one target: Fargo."

"That rings right, but he's a hard man to notch your sights on. When he's out in the open he sticks to cover and seems to know right where we are."

"You're talking ambush from a distance. And there's times when he *ain't* covered. Like when he crosses from the station to the barn. We take that son of a bitch down, Willy, and by the Lord Harry, we'll be drinking from Sweetwater Creek."

"He's got a set of oysters on him," Willy pointed out. "And you're talking about moving in close enough to kill him with one shot. I'm just scairt we might dodge a flood only to step into a stampede."

Kreeger threw up his hands in surrender. "All right, t'hell with you. I don't need no goddamn nancy-boy weak sister siding me anyhow. Just divide up the grub, saddle your horse, and clear out. Fargo took care of the Indian threat, so you can ride out safe to lead a life smoking other men's butts. Me? I aim to leave Fargo colder than a wagon wheel and keep the gold all for myself."

Panic flitted across Willy's rodent features. "Whoa, boss, I never said I was hightailing. You know how I run my mouth sometimes. I'm with you from here to the roundup."

Dub slapped his partner's back. "I knew it all along, Willy boy. A well-bred dog hunts by nature. Don't you fret—we'll kill Fargo, poke them bitches, then carve 'em up until they fork over that gold."

By midday Fargo and Crazy Charlie had hauled both human and animal carcasses well away from Robert's Station. Fargo seldom averted his eyes for long from the rock-strewn slope north of the federal road.

"You figure Kreeger and Hanchon are watching us?" Charlie inquired as he wiped his forehead with a sleeve.

"No bout adoubt it," Fargo replied. "Matter of fact, I figured they'd a tossed lead at us by now. I reckon we're too far away for them to pop over."

Charlie's moon face was suddenly grim with worry. "Might be they'll still try. We're out in the open."

Fargo nodded as both men headed back to the station, Fargo leading the Ovaro. "The criminal mind is too twisted to be predictable. I once cornered a bank robber in Sacramento. He told me he'd surrender if I sent in a hot mince pie. I did, he ate it, and came out with hands up and licking his lips."

"That jasper was crazy," Charlie said. "And I oughter know. Say, Fargo, you said criminals ain't got much guts. You think maybe Kreeger and Hanchon have lit out? Hell, you've done for two of the gang."

Fargo gave that one some thought. "If the only lure around here, for Dub, was Marlene, I'd say they've dusted their hocks. But they've got the gold sickness just as bad as Darlene does. They could be gone, but I'm assuming they're still around. Speaking of dusting hocks . . ." Fargo's lake blue eyes bored into the stock tender. "How come you haven't cut loose from these diggings by now? It can't be the wages."

"I told you—I'm too damn crazy. Crazy for tits. Can you deny these three gals got the finest catheads you ever seen?"

"They rate aces high," Fargo admitted. "But I've never met a man willing to die for a glimpse of a tit."

"Every man chases his own dream," Charlie said piously.

"You're so full of shit, your feet are sliding," Fargo said calmly.

As they neared the stock barn Fargo handed the reins to Charlie. "Don't stall him, old son. Cinch my saddle on him and bring him back outside."

"You're going to ride him? Tempting fate, ain't you?"

Fargo snorted. "Hell, I did that when I decided to stay on at this lunatic ranch. Anyhow, I'm just going to give him a good run, then bring him back. That stallion has got cooped-up fever, and he's likely to kick a wall out if he doesn't run."

Charlie nodded. "Yeah, he's getting testy. Bit me on the ass when I was filling his oat bucket. Anyhow, if he runs like he looks, a Green River sharpshooter couldn't tag him on the fly."

"After you get him rigged, get humping on those two team horses—we need them saddle-broke pronto. I want this place behind me before another Indian welcoming committee stops by."

"I'll do it, boss, but you said you ain't leaving without them yaller boys."

That reminder cankered at Fargo. Seeing Charlie's mock-innocent face tempted Fargo to give him the rough side of his tongue. Instead, he remarked calmly, "Speaking of the gold, right now I'm heading east down the road to search for it. I'd appreciate it if you'd save me the trouble, not to mention the danger."

"You need Darlene, not me."

"I figure she's the mainspring, all right. But being as you're such a spy, I was hoping you'd tell me where it is."

"I only spy on titties. Didja hear about the gal whose tits was so big she lived in two counties?"

"You *know* where that damn color is," Fargo said. "I'm just too softhearted to beat it out of you."

"I don't know one damn thing that's useful," Charlie insisted as he veered into the corral. "I wish I was back in Illinois pulling and burning stumps to clear my old man's land for crops."

"You told me you hailed from Arkansas."

Charlie grinned over his shoulder at Fargo. "Actually I'm from Ohio. See? I'm not only crazy, I'm a shameless liar."

Fargo shook his head in disgust. "God kiss me," he muttered. "I should just grab leather and hightail it."

But he was too mule-stubborn to do the smart thing. Keeping crimped eyes on the slope to his left, Fargo walked another circle around the barn looking for hiding places. But none of the dirt appeared to have been disturbed. Arrows protruded from the barn, and the door was singed from the explosion earlier. Fargo realized they had jumped over a snake that time. More trouble was only a whoop and a holler away now.

He glanced at the sky: past three by the sun. Charlie led the Ovaro out and Fargo stepped up into leather, reining the stallion toward the road. The Ovaro, anticipating wind in his mane, shuddered with eagerness.

Hauling back on the reins to restrain his horse, Fargo first held it to a trot to work out the kinks. Running it full-bore after days in the stall might cause the stallion to pull up lame—a disastrous outcome in rugged mountain country.

Then again, Fargo knew he could be picked off like a louse from a blanket if he lollygagged too long. The moment the Ovaro's gait felt loose and easy, Fargo slapped him on the neck and shouted "Hi-ya! Hii-*ya*!"

The Ovaro shot forward so fast that Fargo felt his feet being pulled from the stirrups. From a trot to a canter to a lope and a gallop, then a blurring run, the Ovaro laid back his ears, lowered himself for the longer strides, and gratefully sucked in huge swallows of the crisp, clean air.

Fargo, too, was suffering from cooped-up fever. At night he didn't like a ceiling coming between him and the stars, and fighting from holed-up positions struck him as the road to hell. He preferred the Indian style of fighting, roving around the battlefield and watching for the main chance. Circling the wagons simply made the attackers' job easier. Wit and wile, that was the key.

Wit and wile had saved them in today's battle. But Dub Kreeger and Willy Hanchon weren't superstitious aborigines. And while it was true that most outlaw hard cases were spineless poltroons, that didn't mean they weren't cunning, dangerous killers.

Thinking all this, Fargo reined in his stallion and wheeled him around, taking him back at a slow trot to cool him out. Fargo knew he was rolling the dice, but the good ground cover didn't start until about six hundred yards up the slope. And the west wind was stiff and steady—anyone shooting at him or his horse would face knotty problems with wind drift.

Along the way Fargo kept a sharp eye out for any potential

117

hiding places for the missing gold. It didn't seem likely to him that it would be hidden out here, but the only places left he could think of were the kitchen and the girls' bedroom. He tilted his hat against the progress of the setting sun, nerves on edge for the sound of a carbine.

But his ride remained peaceful, and that gnawed at Fargo. With Link and Fats cold as a basement floor, had the remaining two changed their tactics? Fargo preferred the devil he knew. Or was Charlie sane for once in suggesting the two had their bellies full and had lit out?

Fargo nixed that idea. Twenty-eight thousand dollars in quarter, half, and double eagles was enough incentive to corrupt a saint. So were three beauties who would turn heads in Paris—especially to a pair of tomcats with no other queens to chase.

He reined in at the stock barn and swung down, then loosed the bridle and dropped the foam-flecked bit. He led the Ovaro inside and stripped the saddle, taking the wet blanket outside to dry in the sun. Crazy Charlie was busy working a team horse, so Fargo rubbed down the Ovaro and ran a currycomb through the witch's bridles in his mane.

"How's it going?" Fargo asked Charlie.

Charlie had placed a blanket on the bay's back to get it used to weight. Now he tossed another one on. "Won't be long and this steed will be broken to bridle or trace. Any trouble out there?"

Fargo shook his head, lost in rumination. He tucked his thumbs behind his shell belt. "Nah. Nothing I can see, anyway."

"Hell, you sound disappointed. Do you *want* trouble?"

"That all depends. What's the good of dodging the fare if we lose our freight?"

Charlie slowly shook his head. "Boss, that's too far north for me. You want to spell it out plain?"

"Yeah. If trouble's bound to come, I druther deal with it sooner than later."

"Is it coming?"

Fargo gave him a pitying look. "Does your mother know you're out?"

Then he headed toward the station house.

18

"What are you doing poking around in the kitchen?" Darlene demanded. "If you're looking for food, it's a forlorn hope. We're dang near out of everything."

Fargo glanced into the oven of the big iron cookstove. "You know what I'm looking for, spitfire. Why'n't you just hand that gold over?"

"And why don't you just stick your dick in your ear and make a jug handle out of it?"

Fargo straightened back up and met her fiery green eyes. "Is that how women talk back in Pennsylvania?"

"Oh, don't come the Dutch uncle with me! It didn't take you three days to screw both my sisters, and them new widows."

"We helped him along," Sharlene reminded her sister.

"With me, it's always the woman's choice," Fargo agreed. He began opening the raw-lumber storage cabinets. Next he turned to a mud chimney that rose from a flagstone hearth. He checked for loose stones and even wedged himself into the chimney and felt around.

"Don't forget to check the spittoons," Darlene barbed.

"Skye," put in Marlene's worried voice, "will them Injins be back?"

"The red man is notional, so it's hard to say for sure. If the council votes for a vengeance quest, they'll be back. But with luck we'll hit the trail before they paint and dance. They'll spend a few days honoring the dead."

Fargo didn't bother to add more ominous news. During his ride back to the stock barn earlier he had seen fresh notches carved into the trees. He knew they were messages from Indian couriers, but no white man had ever broken their code. He wasn't sure which tribes made them, either, but this region was visited by more than the Flathead tribe. Crows, Arapaho, and Blackfeet often escaped here from the blue-bloused pony soldiers, and Fargo had even spotted raiding parties of Apaches and Comanches.

"Who gave you permission to enter our bedroom?" Darlene demanded as Fargo headed for the curtained archway.

"Who gave him permission to save our lives today?" Marlene responded hotly to her sister. "Quit talking to him like he's a dog."

"Cinch your tongue, you sassy bitch! He ain't no law—he's just a drifter hired by the army. In case you ain't never heard, American citizens and their homes can't be searched without a—without a—"

"Warrant," Fargo finished for her. "But you were right the first time—I'm not the law. Since I'm just a private citizen like you, this isn't a search. I'm just poking around."

"Oh, you're an expert at 'poking,' all right," Darlene shot at him spitefully.

"He is," Marlene agreed as they all followed Fargo into the large bedroom. He lifted the chimney of a coal-oil lantern and fired up the wick with a lucifer lying in a clack-dish.

His jaw dropped in astonishment. He was staring at the largest bed he had ever seen. "All three of you sleep in one bed?"

"All *six* of us when our men was alive," Sharlene said. "And none of us was bashful. Our men lifted our nightdresses anytime the mood came over them."

Marlene tittered. "And if they lifted the wrong dress, it didn't matter none. It was all in the family."

Fargo was left speechless by this intelligence. Given how gorgeous all three of these lasses were, he figured this bed must have stayed lively well into the night. For the first time Fargo realized how much those three brothers had lost when they were killed.

"S'matter?" Darlene taunted him. "Does that offend you, long-shanks?"

"Offend, no. Amaze, yes." Fargo dropped to all fours and groped under the bed.

"You just ain't giving up, are you?" Darlene said.

"Nope. I mean to win the horse or lose the saddle—no half measures."

"That sounds like you, all right," Darlene admitted. "You're definitely no halfway man. I wish you was. Maybe then we could . . . come to an understanding."

Fargo moved to the other side of the continent-sized bed and slid under. Nothing but dust bunnies. Holding the lantern, he moved back and forth in a crouch, examining the floor planks.

"You're just washing bricks," Darlene assured him.

"Uh-huh. But tell me this: Since I'm the one leading you gals out of here, how do you figure to sneak that gold out?"

"By then you're going to be a halfway man—you're gonna give over with this strong-jawed crusader bunkum and take your slice of the pie."

Fargo set the lantern back down, watching her. "And just how will you manage that? With me, bribes or bullets usually means bullets."

Darlene flashed him a smile that Fargo felt in his hip pocket. "Maybe you just ain't had a good enough bribe—besides your share of the gold, I mean."

Darlene extended an arm to indicate her sisters. "There's three of us, Skye, and a bed big as a homestead. You ever gonna have an offer better than that?"

"It would be hard to . . . top," he admitted, his tone wistful. "Any one of you girls takes the blue ribbon, but all three . . ." He trailed off, his mind painting vivid pictures. "But what's to keep me from going along with it and then doubling back on you when we reach Fort Seeley?"

Darlene laughed. "That's easy as pie to answer. Any man who won't swear an oath has a code he lives by, and when he gives his word he ain't just chewing his lip. You won't give your word to us unless you mean to keep it."

"So if it isn't bribes," Fargo clarified, "it's bullets?"

Darlene waved this off. "I'd say you're a mighty hard man to kill. I'm counting on the bribes."

"So are we," Sharlene and Marlene said in musical unison, and Fargo felt himself wavering.

Reluctantly he forced himself back to another pressing matter. "We can hash this out later. Ladies, don't get the idea that Dub Kreeger has skedaddled just because two of his men were killed."

"But when you came in," Marlene reminded him, "you said you was surprised that Kreeger and rat face didn't take a shot at you when you was riding. Didn't you mean they was gone?"

"No, sweetie. I think it just means they've come up with a new play. They're holding off on the potshots to make us *think* they've raised dust. Then they plan to move in close and make that play."

"What kind of play?" Darlene wondered.

"Well, killing me would top the list. But grabbing one of you girls would give them a chip and keep their hand in. We're not about to leave here with one of you missing and they know it."

"So what do we do?" Sharlene asked. "We don't go outside much anyhow."

"What about to the privy out back?"

"We've never used that," Darlene spoke up. "Rats. We use chamber pots."

"Hunh," Fargo said idly. "I know there's rats at the base of these mountains, but I never heard of them coming up this high. Well, be careful as all hell if you do go outside. Take a weapon and try not to go alone."

Fargo cast a long glance at Darlene, his weather-bronzed face speculative. He had searched the stock barn, the station house, and along the road for a fair piece in either direction, but no soap—that gold was not in the obvious places. But what possibilities were left? A cliff behind the station cut off any hiding place to the south, and the rock-strewn slope to the north would be tough sledding for women carrying a heavy strongbox.

There was, however, that bathing pool due east from here where he and Jasper Dundee got their first pleasing glimpses of the naked sisters. It would be a long way to haul that strongbox on foot, but amazing things could be accomplished by anyone who'd gone gold simple.

"Something on your mind besides your hat?" Darlene challenged him, fidgeting under his stare.

"I was just remembering when I saw you naked," he replied.

"A pleasant memory?"

"It's tolerable," Fargo admitted.

"See how it is, girls?" Darlene said to her sisters. "All men are tomcats on the prowl. Fargo is starting to see our side of it. The army don't amount to a hill of beans next to what *we* got to offer."

Fargo waited until it was dark outside then slipped out of the station. Hugging the shadow of the building, he crouched for a few minutes just looking and listening.

There were no cicadas or grasshoppers this high up, but the wood-burrowing insects known as deathwatch beetles raised a steady ticking sound. Their spooky racket made Fargo's palms sweat—according to back-country lore they were only heard right before someone died. The wind, always lively up on these slopes, gave off an eerie whistling like kids made when they blew into sarsaparilla bottles.

Knocking off the riding thong, Fargo shucked out his Colt and made a quick circle around the station. Then he sprinted the forty yards or so to the barn. He could hear Crazy Charlie inside bellowing out another of his bawdy tunes:

"Mary had a little lamb,
Its fleece was white as snow,
And everywhere that Mary went,
That lamb would sniff her hole."

Fargo eased past the damaged door and saw Charlie riding one of the team horses up and down.

"Skye Fargo!" Charlie called out. "Well, cut off my legs and call me Shorty! I figured them three gals woulda smothered you in titty flesh by now."

Fargo waved this off. "Making good progress with our new saddle horses, huh?"

"Here's another one gentle enough to carry eggs," Charlie boasted. "I'm a by-God peeler now, Mr. Fargo. Ain't it the berries?"

Fargo could have reminded Charlie that he wasn't exactly starting with wild horses, but he bit back the sarcasm—the disgusting fool was doing a good job at turning that stagecoach team into combination horses, and these horses were the key to putting this place behind them.

"Good work," Fargo said. "Only one left, right?"

"Yessir, that walleyed bay in the middle stall. One more day is all I need."

"Yeah, but don't get so caught up in your work that you forget to keep a sharp eye out. Kreeger and Hanchon know they can stop us by killing those horses."

Charlie tossed back his head and loosed a howl. "It ain't just that, boss. That Dub Kreeger has got a bullet with my name on it."

"Why? Did he catch you staring at *his* tits?"

Charlie laughed so hard he almost slid off the horse. "I don't understand it," he said with exaggerated innocence. "He was shootin' up the place and I just hollered from the loft: 'It's common knowledge that you fuck your mother!' He had a conniption fit."

"Yeah," Fargo said from a deadpan. "Hard to figure in a man who's part Mexer."

Fargo had put in a long day with no sleep the night before, and his muscles felt as numb as his head. He climbed up into the loft with the intention of grabbing a catnap—no more long sleeps until he put paid to this mission. He gathered up some loose straw and made a little pallet next to the loft door, then propped his Henry against the wall and loosened his shell belt.

It bothered him, however, that he had a good view only to the east. There was no way to study the western approach without actually going outside. He stretched out in the hay and shouted below: "Charlie!"

"Yeah?"

"You're watching that door, hey?"

"I ain't herding woollies, boss!"

Fargo wished he was. Sheepherding was a task more his gait. Or *was* he really the dipshit simpleton he appeared to be? He acquitted himself well enough in attacks, and he was doing a first-rate job with those stage-line horses. This was the kind of man, Fargo reminded himself sleepily, that you had to watch in the back-bar mirror.

By now Fargo's eyes felt weighted down with coins and he was balanced on the feather edge between wakefulness and the Land of Nod. He was about to tumble over the threshold into sleep when a noise suddenly jolted him awake.

A fast scratching noise followed by a snort.

The Ovaro. That was the noise it made when it was stutter-stepping in a straw-lined stall after something alarmed him.

Fargo jackknifed to a sitting position. "Charlie!" he bellowed. "Eat dirt *now*!"

Even as Fargo snatched up his six-shooter and thumb-cocked it, a deafening racket of gunfire opened up below. He crossed the loft in three giant strides and spotted two arms protruding through the door, six-gun muzzles spitting orange fire.

Before Fargo could open up, both muzzles swung up toward him and sent deadly lead at him, one bullet grazing his left cheek in a white-hot crease of fire. Fargo belly flopped to the floor of the loft and sent return fire at the attackers. They hightailed it at the first shot, leaving behind a black cloud of powder smoke and the acrid stench of saltpeter.

Fargo wasn't fool enough to go charging after them. These two were wily enough to lay in wait just outside the door and cut him down when he emerged.

"Charlie!" Fargo called down. "You still alive, old son?"

"Thanks to your warning, Mr. Fargo. But I got a load in my pants."

Fargo shook his head as he pushed to his feet. "You know, you don't have to speak *everything* that comes into your head."

"We got a problem, boss. C'mon down."

Fargo did. The big bay Charlie had just been riding lay on the dirt floor of the barn, blood spuming from a hit to its chest.

"That's what they were after," Fargo said. "The easy targets. They know damn good and well we can't leave without horses. Well, I hate like hell to do it, but Jasper Dundee's sorrel is big and strong. We'll have to put the two lightest sisters on it."

"'Fraid not," Charlie gainsaid. "Look in the third stall on the right."

Fargo did and then loosed a string of creative curses no lexicographer back east had ever recorded. Dundee's cavalry sorrel lay slumped on its side, a huge pool of blood still gathering around its head.

"Had to be a stray shot," Fargo mused aloud. "Not that it matters one damn bit—we're short one horse now. Right when we were starting to get up a head of steam."

"They vented our boilers, all right. I'm plumb bumfuzzled what to do now, Mr. Fargo."

Fargo mulled it, pulling on his beard. Jasper's cavalry sorrel had been a strong, well-trained, bullet-savvy horse like the Ovaro. Fargo had counted on the two mounts to lead and steady the others.

Fargo looked at Charlie. "Well, when you can't raise the bridge you have to lower the river."

"You wanna spell that out plain for a soft brain?"

"Way I see it, there's only one source of horseflesh anywhere around here."

Charlie's jaw slacked open. "You don't mean . . . ?"

"Oh, don't I? They killed our mounts, didn't they? It's straight out of the Old Testament, or so I'm told by Bible readers. An eye for an eye and a horse for a horse."

"That ain't what it says, boss."

Fargo flashed a sly grin. "Well, that's what it says now."

19

Telling Charlie to douse the lantern, Fargo slipped cautiously out into the pole corral to study the moonlit surroundings.

"Skye?" Marlene's worried voice called from the station house. "Are you and Charlie all right?"

"Right as rain," Fargo called back. "Tamp down the flap-jaw and shut the door, lass. Our snakes could still be crawling around. You three girls fill your hands."

"They're filled," she assured him before she shut the door.

Fargo's long years of night scouting had trained him to search an area in tight sectors instead of a sweeping view. Methodically, staying low in the grass, he studied the station, the road out front, the steep northern slope, and finally the flatter terrain to the west.

When his eyes finally fixed in a long stare, they were aimed at the abandoned stagecoach just west of the corral.

Was it abandoned? He had heard no rataplan of escaping horses. If, as he suspected, Kreeger had given up on long-distance sniping, he and Hanchon could be hiding inside—a perfect vantage point for their next attempt on his or the horses' lives.

Fargo berated himself for not burning the damn thing earlier. There was no point to scanning the ridges if a man ignored the bushes around him. Leaving his Henry behind, Fargo dropped down on elbows and toes and began a slow, careful crawl toward the dark outline of the coach.

A sudden warning buzz just to his right sent his pulse racing. Fargo spotted a huge, coiled rattler so close he could make out the green spackles on its back. He dared not rise up and pull foot for fear of revealing his position to the killers

127

who might be lurking in that coach, and shooting the rattle-snake would just as likely leave him a gone sucker.

All of this raced through Fargo's mind in an eyeblink. Not given to hand-wringing under pressure, Fargo slid the Arkansas toothpick from its boot sheath. A rattler could strike only the length of its coil, but this one was easily close enough to sink those curved fangs into Fargo. The snake struck at the exact moment Fargo did, and he was barely able to use the knife as a bat to knock it away.

While it was still flat on the ground and beginning to coil again, Fargo neatly chopped the head off. The sinewy body continued to move, but Fargo worried only about the severed head—he had seen decapitated snake heads bite even a full minute after being chopped off. He speared it on the tip of his knife and flipped it away.

One serpent down and possibly two more waiting. Fargo inched his way forward, using the frequent wind gusts to cover the sound of his movement. About six feet away from the offside door of the coach, Fargo alerted like a hound on point. Here was evidence that he was right in his hunch: the ankle-high grass around the door was clearly trampled down. And the bend of the grass told him it was recent—likely this night.

The Trailsman plucked his Colt from the holster and waited for a wind gust before he drew the hammer back to full cock. He covered the final span, rose to a crouch, and wrapped his hand around the door handle.

Fargo took a long breath to steel himself, then flung the door open. The moonlight showed the profile of a man slumped down in the seat. Knowing these butchers had cut down Jasper Dundee in cold blood, Fargo didn't bother with a fair warning: he sent a slug thwacking into the man's head.

Hastily he circled the coach to make sure the second man wasn't lurking nearby. That's three of these puke pails gone under, Fargo rejoiced. But had he plugged Kreeger or the rat-faced Willy Hanchon?

Fargo crossed to the nearside door. Just as he did, the fickle wind shifted and he wrinkled his face in disgust—the putrid stench of death was unmistakable. But that was impossible. It would take days for a dead man to smell this disgusting.

Fargo eased the door open, pausing on the verge of his next breath. A scud of clouds blew away from the buttery moon, and Fargo stared in horror and revulsion at the mutilated face of Captain Jasper Dundee.

"They carved his *eyes* out?" Sharlene said, turning pale at the thought.

Fargo nodded as he gnawed on a heel of cold pone for breakfast. "That and a few other touches."

"That sounds more like Indian work than white men's," Darlene said. "I've read how they carve a man's eyes out so's he'll spend forever blind in the afterlife."

"For a surety," Fargo said. "But no tribe I know of would dig open a grave and haul the body out—that's powerful bad medicine. Indians will mutilate the body of an enemy they kill in battle, but only when it's fresh-killed."

"It's been four days now since the captain was killed," Darlene said. "I reckon he wasn't too fresh."

Fargo lost his appetite at the memory. "Not hardly. I wrapped him in his slicker and buried him out back this morning after me and Charlie hauled out the dead horses. I set fire to that damn coach, too. It shoulda been torched earlier."

"Well if it wasn't savages," Marlene put in, "then it musta been Kreeger and rat face. Ain't nobody else up here."

"It was them sure as sunrise in the morning," Fargo affirmed. "As former soldiers they would know all about Indian-style mutilations."

"But why'd they do it?" Marlene persisted. "Carving the eyes out of a dead man don't make no sense to me."

Fargo grinned. "That's because you and your sisters got more gumption than those two yellow curs realize. They can't breach this station and they know it—they'd get shot to sieves. So they're trying to unstring your nerves and scare you into turning over that gold."

"What about *your* nerves, Mr. Buckskins?" Darlene taunted from the far end of the trestle table. "I don't 'magine that shooting a bullet into a dead friend was a tonic."

"Oh, it's just business," Fargo replied. "This kind of gimcrack foolishness is wasted on me. But that doesn't mean I

129

don't expect trouble to cross our trail. And right now we're two horses shy of what we need to bust loose from these diggings."

"I will *die* before I ride postillion behind that filthy Crazy Charlie," Marlene vowed.

"Same here," Sharlene chimed in. "That filthy goat. If we put him behind, he'll he groping our boobs. If he's in front, he'll be leaning back into 'em. And wherever we ride, he'll be rubbing boogers on us."

"Nobody's riding 'postillion,'" Fargo interrupted, grinning at these outlanders. "A postillion rider sits on the near horse of the leaders to guide the horses drawing a coach. All you girls are talking about is riding double. But without Jasper's horse nobody's riding double, either. That's fine down on the flats, but on the steep trail we'll be riding, we'd be signing our own death warrants. I've seen mules fall to their death on these mountain trails, and a horse isn't as surefooted as a mule."

"Then what do you suggest?" Darlene demanded. "That we all just walk?"

"I'm still working that trail out. But each of us *will* have a horse. Leastways, I hope so. All of you have to be ready soon—the larder is mighty Spartan by now."

"If that means we ain't got much food left," Marlene fretted, "you're right, Skye. It's pinto beans from here on out, and not much of them."

Fargo aimed a sage glance at Darlene, who suddenly took an interest in her folded hands.

"The real sticker," he said, "is that gold. You can stay here and starve, and maybe fight off Kreeger and Hanchon while you do it. But you're never going to get that gold down without my help. You'll be raped, murdered, and lose the gold into the deal."

Darlene raised her defiant green eyes to boldly meet his gaze. "What about my offer? Throw in with us, and all three of us girls are yours. Along with a divvy of the gold. Don't that beat the living hell outta risking your life on two-bit jobs back of beyond?"

"It's one sockdologer of a temptation," Fargo agreed. "But you're a woman in the throes of gold fever, and gold-fever promises only run lip deep. You'll worm your way out of it once you're safely out of these mountains."

"What if we give you your share before we set out?"

Fargo shook his head. "First chance you get, you'll back-shoot me."

Darlene slapped the table petulantly. "Them little quibbles ain't nothing to the matter. The truth is, you're too damn *honest* to cut yourself in. You're bound and determined to return that gold to the damn army."

"I guess that's so. But I'll still make sure you girls get the recovery fee. Twenty-eight hundred dollars is a tidy pile of mazuma. You can buy a nice house in San Francisco for three hundred."

"Stuff!" Darlene snapped. "We could practically own the city with twenty-eight thousand."

"If I don't return that gold," Fargo said patiently, "do you really think the government is just going to forget about you?"

"No, because you'll speak against us and tell them we took the money."

Fargo shook his head. "That I won't do. The federal government has prisons for women, and I don't hold with jugging females. But the army will put a Wells Fargo man on you, and the moment you're caught wearing your new silky-satins and keeping a carriage, your cake will turn to dough."

"Darlene," Marlene spoke up gently, "Skye is right. He's been right all along. How can three sisters whose husbands was lowly station agents just suddenly get rich? We'd have to have a story, and we ain't got a prayer withouten one."

"I think the twenty-eight hundred dollars makes a lot more sense," Sharlene added. "Our husbands woulda had to work here ten years to make that money. We'll just get some fancy feathers and catch us some rich town men."

"Now you're whistling," Fargo approved.

Darlene's face looked confused for the first time since Fargo had met her. "But—"

"Stick your 'butts' back in your pocket," Fargo cut her off. "It's time to fish or cut bait. The Flatheads could return at any time and bring even more warriors. We're down to the scrag end of the food, and hunting is poor shakes up here. Show me where that gold is, Darlene."

She looked at all three of them in turn, biting her lower lip. "All right. I reckon we're at the end of our tether. I'll take you to it."

"Right now?"

Darlene nodded. "It ain't real close, though—it's buried near the bathing pool where you first seen us. We each carried part of it after we tossed the strongbox over the cliff out back."

Marlene said, "But, Darlene—"

"Shut your fish trap!" her oldest sister snapped. "I'm handling this."

Fargo watched her for several moments in speculative silence. "'Pears to me you still haven't flipped over your hole card. What's your grift?"

"Do you want that gold or not, Mr. Fargo?"

"Oh, I want it, straight enough. But so do you and I smell a fox play coming."

"All right, just forget it. You've been after me for days to cooperate, and now that I do you turn on me like a rabid cur. And they say women are fickle."

Fargo expelled a weary sigh. "All right, we'll play this game through. But I'll warn you again—if you try to snuff my wick, there'll be no 'fair sex' folderol. I'll treat you just like I would a man trying to murder me. And even if you manage to put me under, it's curtains for you and your sisters."

"I toyed with the notion of killing you," she admitted, "but that's smoke behind me. Just saddle your horse and I'll take you to the gold."

20

Sprinting quickly to discourage snipers, Fargo returned to the stock barn. Crazy Charlie was working with the remaining team horse. He had blindfolded it and was leading it up and down the barn with a saddle blanket over its back. He carried his Prussian bolt-action rifle, and his nervous eyes kept darting toward the doors.

"You're riding out?" he asked incredulously when he saw Fargo grab his saddle from the rack. "Well, carry me out with tongs!"

"Places to go and promises to keep," Fargo replied. "You stay on the qui vive, hear? I ain't birding you, we're in for six sorts of trouble."

"I'm loaded for bear, hoss. If those outlaws kill one more horse, we're up the creek. Where you headed?"

"Darlene claims she's taking me to the gold. I don't credit that claim, but I spoze I need to let her play her hand."

"She means to kill you," Charlie declared with heartfelt conviction. "Take you to the gold? Brother, that vixen wouldn't give you the sweat off her tits. Yessir, she means to send you across the mountains."

Fargo cinched the girth and checked all of the latigos. Then he quickly inspected the Ovaro's hooves for cracks or loose shoes.

"She might," Fargo allowed. "Maybe she's decided to deal Kreeger and Hanchon into the mix. Maybe she figures they can be controlled with the promise of quiff."

"Well, ain't that true for you, too?"

Fargo grinned. "To a point. But them two must be starved for it by now."

Charlie grinned. "Sure. They been hiding out so long

133

they ain't seen a white woman since the hogs ate the twins. But them two shit-heels could be anywhere out there, and you'll be riding double. Ain't you scairt they might blast you outta the saddle?"

Fargo fastened the throat latch on the Ovaro's bridle. "The thought runs through my mind. But what choice have I got? You won't tell me where that gold is."

Charlie's moon face became a study in innocence. "You can't make pudding out of air. Them bitches don't tell me nothing."

"That I believe. But you're a damn sneaky spy, and you see everything that goes on around here."

Charlie's innocent face turned sly. "Even seen you screwin'."

"You make my point, mooncalf. Turn over your hole card and tell me where that color is."

"My hand to God, Trailsman, I don't know."

"In a pig's ass," Fargo muttered. Out loud he said, "Then at least tell me this. Darlene claims it's buried out near the bathing pool. Is that jake?"

Charlie tossed his head back and howled before reciting: "Jake! Jake! Make no mistake! We gain in herring but lose in hake!"

Fargo stared at him. "Is that some kind of answer or just more shit dribbling over your lips?"

"Just shit dribbling," Charlie replied cheerfully. "I like the word Jake, is all. Hake, you know, is a little fish that lives in the ocean. You see—"

Fargo shook his head in bewilderment and raised one hand. "Turn off the tap, you simple ninny. Or are you?"

Charlie lifted his shoulders. "Me, I just love titties. Big ones, little ones, pointy ones—yum yum, eat 'em up!"

Fargo averted his eyes in disgust when Charlie went mining in his nose. "Keep at it with the horse, and for Christsakes keep watch on the slope and the station yard. You've got a Spencer on the workbench with plenty of ammo, but don't cook it unless you have a clear bead."

Fargo made a long study of the terrain in the late-morning sun before he led the Ovaro out of the barn. The sky over the snowcapped mountain peaks was the pure blue of a gas flame, and the thin air this high up so clear that visibility was perfect. A light, cool breeze feather-tickled his cheeks, and high overhead a vigilant eagle soared on an updraft.

This was the American West Fargo called home, a land of natural dangers and natural beauty, a land scarce on people and with room to swing a cat in. But lately it was being besotted—besotted with ruthless scum like Dub Kreeger and Willy Hanchon, besotted with shady lawyers and greedy tycoons. Mines, sawmills, railroads, soon even the soot-covered manufactories dotting the east—all of this peopling up would force drifters like Fargo to smaller and smaller, more desolate parcels of wilderness.

"We gain in herring but lose in hake," he muttered.

As he led the Ovaro toward the station house, Crazy Charlie's other line nibbled at Fargo's mind: *Jake! Jake! Make no mistake!*

There was no upping-block for women at Robert's Station, and the Ovaro stood seventeen hands high—too tall for Darlene to fork leather on her own. Fargo wrapped his hands around her wasp waist and started to lift her. Then he thought better of it and set her back down.

"What's the matter?" she taunted him. "Ninety-eight pounds too much for you to lift, Mr. Buckskins?"

"I could toss you into the Nevada territory and just might," Fargo replied. "The problem is having you sit behind me. That pretty dress could hide an arsenal—I want to search you first."

Darlene's big wing-shaped eyes sparkled when she laughed. "Fargo, you men are all alike. You just want to feel me up."

"Oh, that'll be a pleasure," Fargo readily admitted. "You got more curves than the Rio Grande. But pleasure ain't the point. You've sent both your sisters to kill me, and this time I expect you to aim to put paid to it yourself."

"My *sisters*," she said, spitting out the word. "Them stupid bitches put a rugged face and a big dingus ahead of twenty-eight thousand dollars. Well, anyhow, I agreed to take you to the money, didn't I? S'matter, you don't trust me?"

"I trust everybody," Fargo replied as he began patting her down. "But I always cut the cards."

She laughed. "Bosh! Is that how's come I cleaned you out

at poker the other night? You didn't get one card from the top of the deck."

Fargo ignored that and finished his search of her remarkable body.

"You didn't check between my tits," she goaded him when he was through. "Ain't you never heard of a tit gun?"

Fargo had indeed and he wasted no time probing one hand into the bodice of her white dress and then the warm cleft between her breasts.

"Like 'em?" she teased in a mean voice.

"Solid and good-sized just like your sisters," he replied, reluctantly pulling his hand back out. "It's easy to see why Crazy Charlie can't see enough of 'em."

"'Cept you won't never suck on these," she vowed as he lifted her onto the hurricane deck. "I wouldn't spread my legs for a goddamn lily-livered man who gives perfectly good gold back to the government."

Fargo stepped up into leather and shook out the reins. "Just my rotten luck, too. Your sisters are right peart, but you cap the climax. Prettiest and shapeliest."

This was a bald-faced lie—Fargo believed all three Stanton girls were right out of the top drawer. But instead of her usual peppery retort, she remained silent this time.

Fargo had chosen the back of the station, with the cliff behind them, for mounting up. Now he dug out his field glasses and nudged the Ovaro to the front corner of the house. Meticulously he scanned the rocky slope rising above them with special attention to the ravines and rock nests. In the background, rugged mountains wearing ermine capes of snow saw-toothed a sky of bottomless blue.

"You're fretting about Kreeger and Hanchon, ain't you?" she said.

"And you aren't?"

"They're just men," Darlene said dismissively.

"Yeah, and what their guns fire are just bullets. Or maybe you plan to talk chummy with them about that gold?"

"That's a libel on me. But anyhow, I expect they wouldn't be so mule stubborn as you."

"I'd call it stubborn when they murdered your husbands," he fired back.

"Ain't you noble?" she taunted him. "Screwing widows before their husbands are cold in the ground. Don't try your pulpit talk on me. I won't swallow your bunk like my sisters will."

Fargo gave it up as a bad job. "Which way?" he finally asked, sliding the glasses into a saddle pocket. His eyes stayed in vigilant motion.

"Head down the federal road until the cliff stops. When you see a hogback on the right, turn off and head toward it. The gold's buried on the backside of that ridge."

"Doesn't sound all that close to the bathing pool," Fargo pointed out.

"It ain't. I lied."

Fargo shook his head in disgust. "Naturally."

Fargo tapped the Ovaro with his heels and they set off at a trot down the road. Darlene wrapped her arms loosely around his waist. Fargo realized the Henry was within reach of her right hand, but the long gun could neither be quickly pulled from the scabbard nor fired for such close-in work. Nor could she easily snatch his Colt because the riding thong was looped over the hammer. And she'd have to lean too far forward and down to grab the Arkansas toothpick.

"Didja mean what you just said?" she asked him.

"You mean when I said 'which way'?"

She punched his arm. "No, you bearded jackass. About me capping the climax?"

"No bout adoubt it. All three of you gals look like Greek goddesses. But *you* are a huckleberry above a persimmon."

"You don't *have* to sugar talk me, you big galoot. I'm taking you to the money."

Fargo believed that about as much as he believed that an Apache could become a Quaker. This wily lass was savvy and ruthless, the type that would shoot a nun for her gold tooth. But he watched only the terrain around them as he replied, "I don't blow smoke about such matters. The first time I laid eyes on you I had to hold my hat in front of my fly."

Darlene's arms snugged a little tighter. Her breath was animal warm and moist on his neck. "Honest Injun?"

"Straight arrow."

He could feel her breasts nudging his back, heavy and firm. Her dress rode well up on her shapely thighs. Fargo nonetheless kept his eyes peeled, watching the rocky terrain around them for movement, not shapes. Kreeger and Hanchon were out there somewhere like circling buzzards.

"This saddle hurts my hinder," she complained. For just a moment Darlene pulled her right arm away from him. When it came back it was around his neck—and a razor-sharp blade pressed against his windpipe.

"Didn't think to search my hair, didja?" she taunted. "This is Marlene's Indian knife, and it'll open your throat like a fish belly."

"You do turn a poetic phrase," Fargo quipped, nervous sweat beading on his forehead. He didn't require the lesson—the knife was carved out of obsidian, a black volcanic glass that could be sharpened finer than iron. He had seen such knives open jugular veins in an eyeblink.

"Big man in buckskins," she roweled him. "Both my little sisters, fresh-made widows with the worms still feasting on their dead husbands. But that don't stop you from dipping your wick in 'em. You'll screw anything that moves, won'tcha?"

"Generally," Fargo corrected her, "I don't limit myself that way."

He was on the verge of sending a hard elbow into her ribs when Darlene burst out laughing and removed the knife from his throat.

"I'm damned if I'll kill a man like you before I've had my use of you. Marlene is always loud in the rut, but any man who can make Sharlene bark like a coyote is a cut above."

"I take a journeyman's pride in my work," Fargo said modestly. "We're off the main road and there's some good rock tumbles around us. Why'n't we hide behind one?"

She brought her lips close to his left ear and shot a tongue into it. "I got a better idea, long-shanks. And we won't even have to stop."

"Damn," Fargo muttered, duly impressed. "But somebody could be glomming us."

"I know," she said as she planted both hands on his shoulders and lifted herself. "I *hope* so. Gets me all exfluctuated. Slide back when I move."

Nimbly, she climbed around front and sat with her butt against the pommel, facing Fargo. He moved high onto the cantle while she hiked her floral-print dress up, giving him an excellent view of her thick bush and the petals and folds of her honey-glistening sex.

"Let's *see* what the girls been taking on about," she announced, untying his fly. "Ain't no man could possibly . . . Great jumpin' Judas!" she exclaimed when Fargo's pulsing member sprang into view, blue veins bulging like fat night crawlers. "Is that a tree limb?"

She gripped his staff and gave it a few pumps. "Well, it fit inside Sharlene and Marlene, so I'm gonna strap it on, too. Lift me up and set me down on it. We'll let your horse do the work."

Like her trim sisters, Darlene weighed less than a memory. Fargo took the reins in his teeth and pulled her over his rigid manhood, both of them gasping with pleasure when he lowered her until he was all the way inside.

The Ovaro, snorting in protest at all this strange motion on his back, nevertheless held a steady trot, and the up-and-down motion kept Darlene moving like a piston on Fargo's man gland. Fargo took a tit in each hand and struck a pleasure lode when he tweaked her nipples with his thumbs.

"Fargo, that's good fixin's!" she cried, squirming like an excited puppy. "Notch that stallion up a bit!"

Fargo, barely able to hold the two of them in the saddle as tight, growing pleasure turned him wobbly, doubted the wisdom of her command. The Ovaro, though well trained, was after all a stallion and given to contrary behavior. Nonetheless, Fargo rolled the dice and gigged him up to a canter. As a result Darlene bobbed up and down on him even faster, shrieking with pleasure.

"Faster, Fargo!" she begged. *"Faster!"*

Fargo, weaving in the saddle like a drunk, opened them out to a lope, and now keeping both of them in the saddle was like trying to ride a rockslide. New levels of pleasure, however, washed away common sense. He was holding on only with his strong legs, but they grew weaker by the second as the she-devil riding his shaft sapped him. Fargo feared a broken neck was in his near future, but he cursed the risk and rode hell for leather.

"Faster!" she cried again between panting gasps, and this time she reached back to slap the Ovaro's neck. The startled and annoyed stallion lengthened his stride to a gallop, and moments later the two randy riders climaxed simultaneously.

The explosive release turned Fargo into a rag doll and he was helpless to prevent it when he and Darlene bounced to the ground and tumbled ass-over-applecart through the knee-high grass of a draw between two steep hills.

"You all right?" Fargo managed when they finally came to a stop.

Darlene sighed. "I ain't never been this all right. That horse of yours puts a bed to shame."

Fargo could see the Ovaro calmly grazing nearby, obviously glad to have the two copulating humans off his back.

Fargo helped her to her feet and whistled the Ovaro in. "What about your notion that the best time to kill a man is when he's getting his shiver?"

"I got to shivering, too. You're one powerful journeyman, sure enough."

Fargo grinned. "You still set on killing me?"

"I ain't sure. This was pleasure, but that money is business."

Fargo snatched the knife from her hair and tucked it behind his shell belt. "There's no strongbox beyond that hogback, is there?"

She wiped grass off her dress and shot him an impish grin. "'Course not. Didja really think there was?"

Fargo matched her grin. "Nah. I just hoped to have a little fun."

"Same here. Let's get back before the girls kill Crazy Charlie. Marlene is fair set to geld him for spying on you and her."

Fargo turned the stirrup and helped her into the saddle, then climbed aboard himself. "All right, but you best make up your mind, girl. I figure we'll be able to ride out of here tomorrow, and if you leave that gold you won't be likely to ride back for it. You'd need to have an escort, and there's nobody you can trust with that much money."

"Nobody," she repeated. "Not even you."

Fargo reined the Ovaro around and gigged him forward. He opened his mouth to reply when the sudden whip-cracking sound of an army carbine rent the peaceful silence of the mountainside.

21

Fargo had beat the survival odds on the frontier by always "riling cool" and staying frosty in the teeth of an attack. With that first shot still whining in his ears, he thumped the Ovaro's ribs hard and the stalwart stallion shot forward as if catapulted.

More shots split the peaceful day, and Fargo immediately set to work following the bullets back to the guns. As low shots sent up plumes of dirt and grass, he calculated the angle and direction of attack.

There were two shooters, almost certainly Dub Kreeger and Willy Hanchon. They were firing from the east flank, about a hundred-fifty yards out, and from ground level—most likely a tumble of rocks Fargo spotted. This was confirmed a moment later when feathers of black smoke curled above the rocks.

"Slide down as far as you can behind the left side of my horse!" Fargo ordered Darlene even as another bullet snapped past only inches from his head. "But hang on to me and don't fall!"

Fargo knew, at this dangerously close range, that firing back would be a fool's play. He couldn't possibly hit hidden men well forted up, nor could he spare the ammo. The best option was to rely on the Ovaro's speed and agility to get him and Darlene out of range.

Despite the Ovaro's impressive speed, however, he dared not simply escape in a straight line—at this range the attackers could easily lead the stallion and fire for score and with the Ovaro shot out from under him, Fargo knew his own life and Darlene's were forfeit. So he led his mount in an unpredictable zigzag pattern, reining hard left, reining hard right, now and then wheeling the Ovaro. During all this he veered steadily to the west, both to open up the distance and to gain the safety of the hogback.

Finally the bullets began ranging wider, and the Ovaro crested the ridge. They plunged to safety down the far side, and Fargo reined in.

"Why we stopping?" Darlene demanded. "We oughter get back to the station before them two run us down."

Fargo slid from the saddle and pulled her down with him. "Nix on that. Outlaws prefer the ambush, not gun battles. I need to find out something."

He pulled his field glasses from a saddle pocket. The Ovaro was lathered, so Fargo loosed the cinch to let him blow.

"That was a fancy piece of riding," Darlene told him as Fargo sprawled in the grass just beneath the crest of the hogback. "'Course, not as fancy as the riding *we* done."

Fargo's white teeth flashed through his crop beard. "That was some pumpkins, sugar britches. I won't ever likely top that."

"Why you watching them?" Darlene asked.

"Horses," Fargo replied cryptically. He focused in on the spot where powder smoke still smudged the clear mountain air.

"How you gonna steal their horses from clear over here?"

"I'm not. But here's the way of it. We started with five healthy horses. These puke pails killed two of 'em. We'll need at least two more if we hope to dust our hocks down onto the flats. Riding double on these shale slopes, and all the broken talus, would be like sitting on dynamite all the way down."

"I see it now. You're watching to see where they go."

Fargo nodded, still peering through the glasses. "They're smart enough to find a new camp after I attacked the old one. Way I kallate it, they should have four horses. Prob'ly in sorry-ass shape, but serviceable mounts."

"But you done for two of the gang—"

"So far," Fargo interrupted, remembering how Jasper Dundee's head had shattered like a clay jar.

"So far. That's two horses they don't need, ain't it? You

142

said the other night that outlaws don't give a tinker's damn about their mounts. Might be they just ate the other two they didn't need. Horse steaks is mighty tasty, and there's damn little meat this high up."

"Yeah, but I'm thinking they will keep these extra mounts on their string. Up here a horse can go permanently lame in a heartbeat, and they'd want remounts."

Fargo watched in silence for a few more minutes while Darlene chewed on a weed. Finally he spotted two horses—a coal black gelding with a roached mane and a strawberry roan—carrying their riders toward the steep, final slope of the mountain.

"They're riding out," he told Darlene. "This might take a while."

It did. Knowing they might be under observation, the two outlaws did everything possible to keep Fargo from charting their progress. They stayed behind whatever cover they could find, rode through draws and coulees, and hid behind the mottes of jack pine and aspen that clung this high up.

"Can you still see 'em?" Darlene asked at one point.

"Thanks to conchos," Fargo replied.

"Conchos? What's them?"

"Silver discs a little bigger than a Mexican peso. For some reason outlaws love to mount them on their saddles. The jasper on the big black—I think it's Kreeger—has a shitload of them. You can't miss the reflections when the sun catches them."

"Kinda stupid for an outlaw, ain't it?"

"I've met very few owlhoots whose strong suit is brains. I was you, I'd keep that in mind before I struck terms with Dub Kreeger. He'll not only take that gold from you, but if he doesn't kill you and your sisters he'll get caught living like a rajah on the money. And the minute he does, he'll bring your name into the mix."

"Kreeger can eat shit and go naked. Did you see me gnashing my teeth when you killed Link and Fats? Them sons a bitches killed three good men in our husbands, and I got my fingers crossed you shoot the other two out from under their hats."

Fargo pulled the field glasses away and glanced at her.

"That doesn't sound like gold lust talking. You having a change of heart?"

Her big green eyes held his clear blue ones. "Wha'd'*you* think?"

They watched each other for another ten seconds before they both broke out laughing.

"Damn," Fargo said. "You're a dangersome woman. You may yet kill me, but I like you."

"And you ain't exactly a poke in the eye with a sharp stick. I sure *hope* I don't have to kill you."

"Same here," Fargo agreed before raising the glasses again. "But I druther kill a woman than a child."

The two outlaws were well up the slope now, moving slowly and occasionally sliding backward a few feet as their horses stepped on unstable surface. Fargo finally lost them when they passed a huge basalt turret, but he had a good fix on their general location. He made a mind map of the spot before he pushed to his feet.

"All right," he said, "it's safe to ride unless the Flatheads are back. Care to take me to that gold now? Time is pushing."

He gave Darlene a hand up. "Time," she said sweetly, "can kiss my ass."

Dub Kreeger and Willy Hanchon stopped to build cigarettes while they let their horses blow. Willy craned his head around to watch the lower slope. "I don't see 'em. Think Fargo is watching us?"

"Scrape the green off your antlers," Kreeger snapped as he licked a paper and quirled the ends. "Are you a bigger fool than God made you? Fargo may be a greasy tumbleweed, but he knows right where he's tumbling. He can't see us now on account a that turret, but he's sighted a plumb line on us."

"Ain't that the drizzlin' shits?" Hanchon complained, backhanding nervous sweat off his forehead. "We'll have to move camp again. He might have more a them damn blasting cans."

"He didn't do so hot with the first one, did he?"

"No, but the second one scared the bejesus outta them savages."

Kreeger snorted. "A puny firecracker will scare off red

144

John. Them ignut gut-eaters ain't even learned how to harness the wheel. Anyhow"—Dub patted his offside saddle bag—"we got a blasting can now, too, thanks to that moon-faced nitwit."

"Yeah, but you just said Fargo knows gee from haw."

"Oh, he's bad medicine, all right," Kreeger said. "Link and Fats are proof of that, and so are them dead Flatheads Fargo scattered over the landscape. But he makes mistakes, too, like not burning that stagecoach sooner. That shot we heard last night was Fargo plugging his own dead pard. And look how easy we got into that barn and done for them horses. Mark me, Willy—if we look for the main chance, before this deal is over, me and you can have the pussy *and* the gold."

Willy shook his head stubbornly. "More likely Fargo will douse our glims."

Kreeger spat onto the rocks, his lean, hard face twisted with scorn. "Reg'lar sunshine peddler, ain't you? Fargo don't put snow in *my* boots. The hell did you expect, Gertrude, a Sunday stroll? We're deserters, desperadoes. We could get bucked out in smoke at any time. Owlhoots like us don't die of old age."

"Maybe not, but they don't die any sooner than they have to, neither. I ain't so sure them three bitches even *got* the gold. And you seen it with your own eyes just now—Fargo pounding Darlene like a spike maul. What if the skirts are dealing him in?"

At this reminder Kreeger's eyes grew smoky with rage. "Yeah, you struck a lode there. Now that's a queer deal. What in pluperfect hell is that bitch up to, gettin' chummy with a crusader like Fargo? Sure, he's been jugged for fighting and whoring on Sunday and such, and he's no scrubbed angel. But he sure's hell ain't gonna help them heist that gelt."

"Maybe, maybe not," Willy said. "T'hell with the newspaper hokum. All that cunny, right outta the top drawer, could turn me honest—why not turn Fargo crooked?"

Kreeger acknowledged that truism with a grunt. "He's likely already poked Marlene, too, and I was saving her for myself. I ain't keen on taking Fargo's leavings."

"That ain't the point. We was talking about striking terms with the sisters and getting a share of the gold, if they got it. We sure's hell can't sugar-talk them with Fargo slipping the cod to 'em."

"Ahuh." Dub Kreeger mulled something for a moment. "Like you said, *if* they got the gold. What if they ain't? By the time we happened on them brothers and killed them, somebody sure's hell had it. Hell, Injuns coulda took that strongbox just to see what was in it."

Willy nodded. "Sure. Looks like they hauled off the bodies of the driver and shotgun messenger. They never turned up."

"We'll have to watch close for that gold," Dub decided, flipping his butt away in a wide arc. "They have to be scraping the gravy skillet by now—hunger will force them to head toward Fort Seeley pretty damn quick. That much gold will be noticeable. We'll have to watch for the main chance and kill Fargo—he's the keys to the mint."

"And if they ain't got the gold?"

Kreeger bared two rows of teeth like crooked yellow gravestones. "Then we still kill Fargo. We won't have twenty-eight thousand in gold cartwheels, but we'll still earn enough to live high on the hog."

Hanchon cast him a curious, sidelong glance, his little red rodent eyes bright with interest. "What's the pitch?"

"You heard of Reynosa?"

Willy shook his head.

"It's a town down in Mexico just south of Texas. I was down there a few years back running slaves. Anyhow, there's a rich Mexer rancher who will pay five thousand dollars for Fargo's head pickled in brine."

"Christ! Don't tell me—Fargo screwed his wife."

"Nah. Poker game. The chilipep got hot when Fargo won a big hand. Jumped up quick and drew down on him. Way I heard it, Fargo had no time to clear his holster or the top of the table. So he swiveled his holster up, shot through the tabletop, and blew the Mexer's left nut right out of the sac— gelded him for life before he had any kids."

Willy rubbed his chin. "It'd be a long, dangerous ride into Old Mex. But, hell, it's dangerous everywhere we go. And five thousand ain't chicken feed. Either way, though, we got to kill Fargo."

Kreeger checked his cinches and then gave Willy a pitying look. "True, but face it, chumley—that's been the way it is ever since we popped over Captain Dundee. Fargo won't leave these mountains while we're above the horizon. And he won't let us leave, neither. Right now he's the Wrath."

Willy took up the reins and swung aboard his strawberry roan. "I guess that's so," he said glumly. "Of all the goddamn swaggering, straight-shooting, blade-running, hard-fisted sons of bitches in all the West, we have to cross sabers with Skye Fargo. It cankers at my gut."

"Mine, too," Kreeger admitted. "I usually don't step in something I can't wipe off. If we'd a recognized him in time, Dundee would still be alive and Fargo might be too busy playing hide-the-picket-pin with them beauties to go on a vendetta against us."

"You lost me on 'vendetta,'" Willy admitted, "but I can guess it. Well, we best get back and move camp."

Kreeger grabbed the roan's bridle, holding Willy in place. He shook his head. "We leave that camp right where it is."

"Dub, have you been chewing on peyote? There's only two of us now, and you just said Fargo's got a plumb line to our camp. He's got to even the score for Dundee, so he *will* be coming."

Kreeger nodded. "With a bone in his teeth. And not just to kill us—he'll want horses. Him and that soft brain hauled out two dead horses from the barn—way I cipher it, they need at least two more to ride out from here. We'll use Link's and Fats' mounts as bait in the trap and keep ours well hidden."

Willy chewed his lower lip nervously. "Well . . . we hafta shit or get off the pot, I reckon. But, say, we can't bollix it up this time. How many chances does a man get to kill Skye Fargo?"

22

Fargo stared at Crazy Charlie. "You wanna say that one more time before I unscrew your head?"

Charlie raised a finger to his nose and Fargo knocked down his arm.

"Talk out, Tumbledown Dick," Fargo snarled.

"You don't threaten them three whores, and *they* don't talk out."

Fargo grabbed a handful of Charlie's shirt and twisted it. "Chuck the sass and give," he ordered in a low, dangerous voice that brooked no defiance.

"Sass? Why, I take no sass but sarsaparilla. You know who said that?"

Fargo tightened his hold and lifted Charlie right off the floor. "I'm on the ragged edge, old son, and in no mood for barroom josh. What did you just tell me?"

"I said Kreeger and the rat face got one of our blasting cans. It was right after you and Darlene rode out. I saw 'em sneaking down the slope toward the barn. I 'membered what you said 'bout not wasting bullets. So when they was close enough to throw at, I lit up one a the cans and sailed it out at 'em. But I didn't wait for the fuse to get burning good like you told me, and it went out soon's I throwed the can. Dub scooped it up and they both lit out."

Fargo got hold of his temper before he spoke. "Charlie, I told you to go ahead and shoot if you had a good target. If you could reach them with a throw, sure's hell you coulda plinked 'em with a bullet."

Charlie's eyes ran from Fargo's. "Yeah. I just wanted to throw the can. I like the noise and the smoke."

Fargo paced up and down in the barn, still watching the stock tender. "Christ, you are a holy show. Now those two scrotes have an extra weapon against us, and being ex-soldiers they know the best way to use it. Well, give me that last can. Hell, you'll sell it to the Indians."

Charlie rummaged in a storage bin and handed the can to Fargo, who stuffed it into his possibles bag.

"I didn't mean to gum up the works," Charlie said contritely. "When I seen 'em so close, I got all boil-brained and just wanted to blow them two to hell."

Fargo, who never stayed hot under the collar long, nodded. "It's too dead to skin now, old son. Now we know these two plug-uglies got that can and we'll have to keep a sharp eye out for it. Did they fire at you?"

Charlie shook his head. "When they realized I'd spotted 'em, they just hightailed it to their horses. Looked like they rode off after you and Darlene."

"I think I see the way of it," Fargo mused aloud. "After I rode out, their first plan was to plug some more horses. But it was broad daylight, and once you jumped into the game at such close range they got chicken guts and decided to follow me and Darlene. Well, at least you choused 'em off before they killed any more horses. But *horses* are still the main mile, Charlie, and it's up to me and you to grab at least two."

"Me, grab 'em?" Charlie repeated, rolling his eyes in shock. "You're mighty mistaken, Mr. Fargo. I can feed 'em, currycomb 'em, and even turn a team horse into a combination horse. But stealing 'em from an outlaw camp is your bailiwick. I'm a drooling idiot."

"Balls! That's a stage play you're putting on to hide some master plan. No drooling idiot could've stayed alive this long out in this barn with warpath Indians and cutthroat killers attacking it."

While he spoke, Fargo had drifted to the barn doors and was studying the surface turmoil of the rock slope.

"I've watched you with horses, Charlie. You're a top hand. You've been around them a long time. That gives a man a permanent horse smell that doesn't come from just riding one mount like I do. If we can find their horses up there, they're gonna be spooked by strangers. But a stranger who's lived with horses will have a better chance of tossing a rope halter on them and leading them down."

"The horses ain't the problem. It's the men and the guns. You've spent much of your life breathing powder smoke, Mr. Fargo. Me, I'm a hay-forker."

"Uh-huh. A hay-forker with a Prussian bolt-action rifle. Anyhow, I'm not asking you to do any work in a shooting affray—I'll take care of that. You won't even be lugging your rifle although you will strap on a short iron in case the pot boils over. Get one from the house. I'll handle the shooting, you handle the horses. Agreed?"

Charlie's round face was so white he looked as if he'd been drained by leeches. But he nodded agreement. "I ain't no hero, but it's come down to the nut-cuttin'. Grub's almost gone, ammo's petering out, and them Flatheads won't be painting and dancing for war much longer. We going tonight?"

Fargo nodded. He noticed how, all of an instant, Charlie had lost his simpleton expression and had spoken sensibly.

"Tonight," Fargo affirmed, "once the polestar is high and the full moon is overhead. This won't be a trip to Santa's lap. They expect me, at least, and there'll be some kind of ambush set up. I want you to wear dark clothes and to smear your face with axle grease to cut down reflection. Stay away from the popskull. And before we leave, we're both going to wrap our heads in blankets."

Charlie cocked his head, curious. "The hell for?"

"Where you been grazing, Western man? A half hour in total darkness prepares the eyes for night vision. You'll see twice as much up on that mountain."

"Huh. I druther stay down here and spy through them loopholes, maybe see some titties."

"Tell you what," Fargo promised as he headed out the doors. "You do a good job tonight and I'll ask all three of the sisters to hang out their wares for you."

Charlie perked up. "Straight goods?"

"Square deal."

"Can I squeeze 'em, too?"

Fargo stopped and turned around. "When a man gives

you bread, don't demand toast. Just keep working on that last horse until I come get you. With luck we'll be riding out of here tomorrow."

"What about the gold?"

Fargo studied him a long time until Charlie was fidgeting nervously.

"Yeah," the Trailsman said before turning around, "what about the gold?"

Under the sterling moonlight Fargo led the way east along the federal road. His Henry dangled in his right hand. Crazy Charlie Waites followed in single file carrying two rope halters he had fashioned earlier. Fargo knew it would be hard enough to handle two nervous horses on that treacherous slope, but he hoped to throat slash the other two. That would effectively end any threat from Dub Kreeger and Willy Hanchon.

But he had not forgotten the promise made over Jasper Dundee's grave: to send *all* of Kreeger's gang to the burning pit.

"How high up you figure they are?" Charlie said in a low voice behind him.

"How long is a piece of string? I know about where they went up, but not how high."

"Sure, it don't matter to you. You're strong as horseradish. But I ain't no rugged frontier type like you. That slope is mighty steep."

"The trip back will be easier," Fargo told him, knowing it was a lie. The trip down was far more dangerous, especially in the dark.

"So you think they're waiting for us, huh?"

"They'd be fools not to. Look, quit pesticating me why'n'cha? Take some deep breaths and settle down. We'll find out short meter what we're up against. These are greasy-sack outlaws, not Cheyenne Dog Soldiers."

"You're the one," Charlie persisted, "who said it's best to look before we wade in. It's only natural I'd want to know what's waiting for us up on that mountain."

"We'll ford that river when we get to it. Sure, I prefer to scout before I lock horns with an enemy. And we'll take a careful squint around when we locate these two shit heels. But this has to be done on the fly and that means accepting some risk. Why do you care anyhow? You're crazy, remember? Crazy men can't be scared."

"Crazy don't mean stupid. I'm sane enough to see that you mean to get my life over."

Fargo spun around so quickly that Charlie bumped into him. "I said put a stopper on your gob. I ain't *even* gonna say it again."

Charlie scowled in the moonlight but finally fell silent. They reached the spot where, yesterday, Fargo had watched the two owlhoots ascend the slope. Fargo gave his companion some quick pointers on climbing loose shale and talus.

"And keep that finger out of your nose," he snapped. "You might need both hands to grab hold of something."

Fargo slung his rifle across his back and both men started the hard scrabble upward. Fargo was quickly impressed: Charlie was nimble and quick and had little trouble keeping up with him.

Fargo realized once again that his sneaky little companion had been hiding his lights under a bushel. A good marksman, a good mountain climber, and a top hand at handling horses. Was he also good at handling gold? But no—Darlene surely had to have it. Charlie was just along for the tits . . .

Fargo paused to wave his hat in front of his face. Even this high up, with flies and mosquitoes absent, gnats swarmed his face and worked into his eyes. Charlie, too, was muttering curses.

"Damn it all, Fargo, the more I sweat the more it draws these little sons of bitches."

Fargo pulled a clean bandana from his hip pocket. "Wipe your face with this now and then. But push these gnats from your mind—you start steaming over them and you might miss the death blow until it's too late."

The two men climbed higher, finally passing the basalt turret. Fargo hoped it wasn't much farther to contact with Kreeger and Hanchon. He preferred a hot-lead showdown to these bloody knees and elbows and aching back.

Higher yet the men scrambled, and Fargo could hear Charlie blowing almost like a horse. Fargo signaled a rest, badly winded himself, and the two men crouched behind small boulders. The wind ripped around in hard gusts this high up, drying the sweat but also reducing them to shivers.

Fargo was about to start forward again when both men heard it: the nickering of a horse somewhere above them.

"Follow me," Fargo said low in Charlie's ear, "and watch for my signals. This is going to be a trap, so just lay low until I draw out the pus."

Adequate ground cover was scarce as they moved up the slope, but Fargo used what was there well. He led the two men wriggling through runoff seams and declivities. Ten minutes later they popped their heads cautiously up from behind a slag heap and spotted two horses in the moonlight: a sorrel and a dapple gray.

Fargo spoke close in Charlie's ear. "Trap, all right. Those aren't the mounts Dub and Willy were riding when they ambushed me and Darlene. These must be Link and Fats' horses."

"We going for all four?" Charlie whispered back. "I can fashion a lead line."

Fargo shook his head. "The other two will be hid a far piece from here. If we spot 'em, sure, let's grab 'em if we can. Or kill 'em if we can't. But right now I have to reconnoiter. Those two shit stains have to be hiding close by. Stay right here until I give the hail."

It was trickier work now. If the wind shifted Fargo's man scent into the horses' nostrils, the resulting whinnies would alert Kreeger and Hanchon. But Fargo had to get closer to figure out where they might be holed up.

"Pile on the agony," he muttered as he moved forward.

Finally, ensconced in a jagged heap of broken rock, he had a good view of a teacup-shaped hollow on the mountainside. The two horses were almost dead center in it with a fairly uncluttered patch of graze around them. But the rim of the hollow was an almost unbroken ring of large boulders.

Fargo felt his heart sink. He didn't mind being the meat that feeds the tiger by exposing himself to view—he had to pinpoint muzzle flash before he could return any accurate fire. But he wouldn't have a snowball's chance of scoring a hit.

Fargo saw how it was and decided on speed over sneaking. Those horses had their bridles on, thrown for grazing. If he could get in there fast, grab hold of them, and get them down to Charlie, he could wage a running battle relying on the Henry's superior magazine.

Fargo rose and dashed across the grassy hollow, expecting guns to erupt. But a scud of clouds had blown over the moon, and the darkness was deeper than moments before. The Trailsman, on the verge of rejoicing, reached both horses and caught hold of them with little trouble. Outlaw mounts were often beaten into submission, and these barely resisted when he started to turn them.

Just then his reckless plan collapsed into total chaos. From the slope behind Fargo, where Charlie was waiting, a gunshot shattered the stillness of the night.

"Hell's a-poppin'!" shouted a voice from behind the rocks, and suddenly Fargo was the turkey in a vicious hail of carbine fire.

23

Cursing Crazy Charlie, Fargo tucked and rolled, coming up on his knees. He could see two muzzles spitting fire, but both outlaws were covered down. Desperate but clearheaded, Fargo shook the Henry off his back and threw it into the offhand kneeling position. He despaired of a direct hit, but with all those boulders behind the shooters, he could set up deadly ricochet.

But he drew another low card when, after only one shot, a cartridge got wedged in the ejector port. A blockage like this took too long to clear, and Fargo was forced to drop the Henry and shuck out his Colt. By this time bullets were zipping past his ears with a deadly drone. He fanned the Colt's hammer, sending in a rapid string of shots.

"Down in front, Fargo!" Crazy Charlie called out close behind him, unable to spot Fargo in the dark.

Fargo bent forward while Charlie sent in five shots, the sixth having been spent already in starting this fray. This combined stream of lead sent both outlaws down behind cover, but Fargo knew they were reloading their Spencers while the two attackers didn't have a shot between them. He was about to give the order to retreat when he remembered that blasting can in his possibles bag.

Moving quickly, Fargo pulled out the can and a lucifer, thumb-scratching it to life.

"Suck on this, Fargo!" a snarling voice shouted just as the carbines began to speak their piece again.

Bullets zwipping through his clothing and ruffling his hair, Fargo lit the shortened fuse and stood up. He aimed between the two fire-belching muzzles and, tossing in a high arc to drop the can in behind the boulders, lobbed it in on a hope and a prayer.

At first, nothing. Fargo opened his mouth to sound the retreat when the clearing suddenly lit up like high noon. A concussive blast rocked the ground under his feet and sent rock fragments hurtling. Flames whooshed to life behind the boulders, casting eerie, distorted shadows.

Then, for perhaps ten seconds, a silence as deep as the tomb. This silence was suddenly broken by a hideous shriek of pain that raised the fine hairs on Fargo's forearms. He moved quickly around the boulders and saw Dub Kreeger crumpled on the ground, dead as a dried herring. Hanchon lay writhing beside him, half his face burned down to bone.

Fargo used one of the carbines to toss a finishing shot into rat-face's brain. Then he turned to confront Crazy Charlie. "So you fired a warning shot, eh, to get me killed?"

"Fargo, my hand to God I didn't! I pulled this Remington out to palm the wheel, and the son of a sorry-assed bitch went off! Honest to John, that's all I done!"

Fargo started to retort, then stopped a moment to think. "Remington, you say? Did one of the girls give it to you?"

"Sure, that witch Darlene."

Fargo couldn't help a tired grin at the woman's vindictiveness. "Charlie, that's the Remington with the worn sear. Hair-trigger. She gave it to you on purpose. Well, you got some starch in your collar after all. Those shots you fired gave me just enough time to toss that can."

"Both dead, huh?"

"They'll be getting their mail delivered by moles. All right, let's halter these horses. I'm too damn tired to look for the other two. I expect Indians will liberate them before too long. They keep a close eye on these mountains."

"We done it!" Charlie said, adding a whoop. "Drove off the red arabs and killed off the Kreeger gang!"

"No need to tack up bunting just yet," Fargo warned. "It's a long ride down to the flats, and on a hard trail."

"So we light out later today," Charlie said. "What about that gold?"

"I s'pose that's up to Darlene," Fargo said. "I was paid to bring those girls back, and she's going with or without it."

Fargo, interested in keeping an eye on Darlene's activities during these final hours, spread his blanket on the hard floor of the station house and caught a few hours of fitful sleep. When he rolled out, back aching, it was late in the forenoon. All three sisters sat at the trestle table, watching him.

"S'matter?" Fargo asked, pushing to his feet and buckling on his gun belt. "Do I snore?"

"That's pee doodles," Darlene said impatiently, her face a mask of barely controlled fury. "Crazy Charlie is gone."

Fargo scrubbed his face with his hands, trying to wake up. "Gone? You sure? He headed for the barn when we came back."

"Oh, he's gone, all right," Darlene said. "So is one of them team horses he broke to the saddle. And if *you* wasn't so damn worried about watching me, you coulda stopped him before he lit out *with all the gold*."

Fargo flinched as if he'd been slapped. "Charlie? Charlie heisted the gold?"

Darlene pointed to a far corner and Fargo did a double take: a small strongbox sat there, the hasp on its lock filed open.

"The box was where I hid it, but he musta had the gold all along, that sneaky little bastard. It's filled with rocks so it feels heavy. We had it hid in the privy out back, down one of the holes. He musta been spyin' on us when we done it. By now he's way to hellangone."

When Fargo's shocked amazement passed, he felt a grudging admiration for "Crazy" Charlie. "Why, that cunning son of a bitch. He kept it dark from everybody all this time. 'Jake! Jake! Make no mistake!' That rhyme *was* a clue. He meant jakes, a privy."

"What rhyme?" Sharlene asked, her pretty face baffled. But Fargo waved off her question.

Darlene stamped her foot. "Fargo, how can you grin about it?"

"It all ciphers," Fargo admitted, ignoring her pique. "All along the four of us figured he didn't have the mentality for it. But he kept us all flummoxed. He knows his hay foot from his straw foot, all right."

Sharlene scowled. "All that time, him watching us and pretending he only wanted to see our tits. That's a hoot!"

Fargo shook his head. "No, lady, that wasn't for show. He coulda left before this. I think he really wanted to see your charms. It's not likely he's ever been around women as fetching as you three."

This compliment drew a smile from Marlene. "Maybe we oughtn't to've been so mean to him. Maybe he'd a gone shares with us."

Darlene scowled at Fargo. "You! You're s'posed to be so smart. Why didn't you twig his game?"

"I wondered about him," Fargo said. "The problem is, I don't trust you any farther than I can toss a biscuit. If you woulda told the truth now and then, maybe I woulda been more suspicious of Charlie."

"You just gonna let him get away with it?"

"No need to slip your traces. I'll track him down. But first I'm getting you ladies back to Fort Seeley. Be ready to ride in thirty minutes. I'll tack the horses."

The outlaw mounts were nervous but docile, the remaining team horse still skittish under the saddle. Fargo let Marlene ride the Ovaro and took the team horse himself. He grained all four horses good, let them tank up from the trough, and tied a bag of crushed barley to the Ovaro's saddle horn for the trail. The humans didn't fare so well, making do with jerky and dried fruit.

Fargo soon left the new federal road, knowing it was patrolled by various tribes and the occasional gang of road bandits. He led them down the south slope of the mountain along an old Indian trace taken over by mountain men until the 1840s. It was narrow and at times steep, twisting and turning like the Platte River.

Darlene pouted the whole time, casting Fargo murderous glances.

"Why you sore at me?" he called out. "I didn't take the damn gold."

"So you say. How do I know you and Charlie ain't in cahoots?"

Fargo measured out a long sigh. "Well I reckon it's out now. See, every time Charlie picked his nose, that was our secret signal."

Sharlene and Marlene giggled. Darlene flounced in the saddle and almost fell off her horse.

As they gradually wended their way lower and the day advanced, the sun took on heat and weight. Pine trees grew thicker now, and Fargo kept a constant weather eye out for ambushers. Not long before sunset they were past the midway point, and blue splashes of wild columbine dotted the slope.

"Dark will set in fast, ladies," Fargo announced. "This little clearing is in the lee of the wind and there's a seep spring. Let's pitch camp."

Fargo dug a fire pit in case of nearby Indians and lined it with crumbled bark from his saddle pocket, kindling a small fire. They boiled some coffee beans and soaked the last of Jasper Dundee's hardtack in it. Fargo fed the horses from his hat and let them drink before tethering them nearby.

"Best to turn in," he suggested. "I want to get off this mountain as soon as we can. By now Indian runners may have reported us to the main gather."

"You gonna sneak off, too?" Darlene taunted him as she spread her blanket. "Join your partner?"

"Sell your ass," was all Fargo said as he rolled into his blanket, listening to the fire snap and pop as it burned down.

During the night a panther screamed nearby. Moments later Marlene showed up at his bedroll. "Skye, I'm scared. Can I crawl in with you?"

Fargo grinned in the darkness as he pulled her in. Not long after Marlene, now ready for deep sleep, returned to her blanket a timber wolf howled mournfully. Seconds later Sharlene showed up. "Skye, can I crawl in? Wolves scare me."

Fargo, ever the gentleman, obliged her. Like her sister she returned to her blanket in a dreamy daze.

"You won't get no more from me, gold stealer," Darlene called out of the darkness. "You and Charlie already screwed me."

"I'm glad to hear that," Fargo assured her. "I'm not sure I'd be . . . up to it."

Sunrise was still a streak of flame on the horizon when Fargo and his three beautiful charges resumed their trek. By late morning they were off the mountain and only five miles from Fort Seeley. They debouched from a thick stand of aspen and Fargo reined in the combination horse, staring in slack-jawed disbelief.

Crazy Charlie stood waiting for them, one finger far up his nose. The saddlebags at his feet spilled brilliant gold coins. His free hand held the hair-trigger Remington aimed at them.

"Fargo, you said if I went up the mountain with you to get horses you'd have all three girls show me their tits. Well, it's gold for tits."

"Open your dresses, girls," Darlene commanded, fingers already flying on her buttons.

Charlie enjoyed this show of luscious pulchritude and finally nodded.

"Don't lower that gun, Charlie," Darlene cautioned urgently. "Fargo will take the gold."

"He'll take it anyhow," Charlie gloated. "Tell 'em why, Fargo."

Fargo had been grinning ever since spotting the Remington. "Because, fair maidens, Charlie only had six bullets for that revolver, and he fired 'em all on the mountain."

Darlene turned dark with rage. "You mean . . . ?"

Fargo nodded. "Charlie screwed you again—the *crazy* bastard."

LOOKING FORWARD!
The following is the opening
section of the next novel in the exciting
Trailsman series from Signet:

TRAILSMAN #365
HIGH COUNTRY GREED

*High in the Rockies, 1861—a wild town where greed is the
way of life and a pack of killers run roughshod.*

Buzzards led Fargo to the bodies. He was bound for the
Rockies and happened to gaze into the sky to the south and
there they were, half a dozen large black Vs winging in close
circles. It could be anything that brought them. A dead animal was most likely.

Fargo was far from any settlements and there wasn't a
farm or a ranch within hundreds of miles. But he had a
hunch and he had learned long ago not to ignore his gut
instincts.

Reining the Ovaro toward the carrion eaters, he loosened
the Colt in its holster.

Fargo was a big man. He nearly always wore buckskins
and always had a red bandana around his throat. His boots
were scuffed, his spurs well worn. Jutting from his saddle
scabbard was the stock of a Henry rifle. In his boot he had an
Arkansas toothpick.

Excerpt from HIGH COUNTRY GREED

His piercing lake blue eyes took in everything. Only a fool let down his guard in the wild and Fargo was no fool.

This was Indian country, mainly Cheyenne and Arapaho. A few months ago a treaty had been signed that would put them on reservations and open the land to whites. Neither tribe was happy about it. They argued that the government had tricked a handful of leaders into signing the treaty without the consent of the rest.

Fargo came to a low rise and saw the bodies. There were two, sprawled belly-down in the grotesque postures of death. Both wore buckskins. As he approached he saw that both had black hair past their shoulders and wore moccasins.

"Hell," Fargo said.

Rising in the stirrups he scanned the prairie in all directions. Other than a few antelope to the northwest—and the vultures—he was the only living creature.

He rode in a circle around the dead warriors. Tracks showed where five riders on shod mounts had come out of the south. More tracks showed where the five shod mounts went off to the west, leading two unshod horses.

The killers had made no attempt to hide their sign.

His saddle creaking under him, Fargo dismounted. Few flies had gathered, which told him the bodies hadn't been there long. Using the tip of his right boot he rolled one over.

It was a young Arapaho who had barely seen twenty winters. A slug had taken him in the left eye and exited out his right temple. The other one had been shot in the forehead. Neither had been mutilated.

Fargo gazed to the west. The five whites who killed the warriors were heading toward the far distant Rockies. He took up their trail.

Fargo wasn't the law. He had no legal right to go after them. But he'd like to know why they did it.

Had the warriors attacked them? Or was it something else?

It was common for a lot of whites to hate the red man simply because Indians were red and for a lot of Indians to hate the white man because the white man wasn't red.

Fargo couldn't abide the haters on either side.

Before him stretched the vast prairie. So much space, you'd think the white man and the red man could live on it in peace, but that would never be.

A sentinel prairie dog atop its burrow whistled shrilly and the whole town scurried for cover.

Fargo reined wide of the mounds and the holes. He was too fond of the Ovaro to risk a busted leg.

The sun was hot, the smell of the grass and the earth always in his nose. He came on a trickle of a creek with banks three feet high. The bottom was choked with brambles and brush. He started down and spooked a small black bear that bolted up the other side and stopped to stare in bewilderment, and snort. He laughed, and the bear loped along the bank and disappeared into more growth.

A half mile on and he spooked a rabbit. It bounded twenty yards or so and stopped to glance back and see if he was after it. He almost shucked the Henry to have rabbit stew for supper. But hardly did the notion cross his mind than the air whistled to the streak of a feathered predator and a hawk dived out of the clear blue. There was a frightened squeal and a brief flutter of wings and a thrashing of legs, and the rabbit lay limp. The hawk looked at him, tilting its head from side to side, as if daring him to try and steal its meal.

"It's all yours," Fargo said.

A thin bowl of sun was all that was left when Fargo spied gray snakes coiling into the sky. He put his hand on his Colt and went on at a walk.

Their fire was too big; a common mistake of those green behind the ears. They were seated around it jawing and drinking coffee and must have had their ears stopped with wax because they didn't hear him until he was almost on top of them.

There were four, not five. Fargo figured the tracks of the fifth shod horse belonged to a pack animal.

Suddenly one of them bleated a warning and all four grabbed rifles and sprang to their feet with the alacrity of men who feared they might take arrows.

"Howdy, gents," Fargo said amiably as he drew rein. He leaned on his saddle horn. "Saw your fire and reckoned you might share a cup."

All four were middling in age, which surprised Fargo; he'd thought they would be younger. Two had bristly beards and two didn't. Their clothes were a mix of homespun and store-bought that had seen better days. Only two wore revolvers but all of them had rifles and knives.

"Damn it to hell, mister," the bulkier of the bearded pair exclaimed. "You shouldn't ought to sneak up on folks like that."

Fargo gestured at the open prairie. "You call this sneaking?"

A smooth-chinned rake handle with tufts of hair poking out of his ears chortled. "He's got you there, Rafer. That we didn't see him is our own damn fault."

"We were damn careless," said the other bearded specimen.

"I reckon so, Milton," hairy-ears said.

"Can I light or not?" Fargo asked, and when the man called Milton nodded, he slid off and stretched.

"Been ridin' a far piece, have you?" asked hairy-ears.

"Clear from Saint Louis," Fargo said. He let the reins dangle and rummaged in a saddlebag for his tin cup. "How about you gents?"

"We're from down Kansas way," said hairy-ears. "My name is Alonzo, by the way." He pointed at the last of them, whose chin was cleft so deeply he appeared to have two. "And that there is Elias."

Fargo stepped to their fire. The coffeepot was half full. He filled his cup, took a step back, and squatted. "I take it by your clothes you must be farmers."

Alonzo bobbed his head. "That we are. Although maybe it should rightly be that we *were*. We've given up the plow to get rich."

"Are you fixing to rob banks?"

Alonzo laughed. Hunkering, he rested his rifle across his thighs. "I would if I thought we could get away with it. But I ain't hankerin' to be guest of honor at a strangulation jig."

"I bet we could do it," Rafer said. "We're smarter than most who pin on badges."

"We'd strike fast, then hide way off where no one is liable to find us," Milton added his two bits. "We're real good at livin' off the land."

"How are you at killing Indians?" Fargo casually threw in. He sipped and stared into his cup and when he looked up, all four were staring at him as if he were a rattler about to bite.

"Why'd you want to bring up a thing like that?" Alonzo asked.

"I came across a couple of Arapaho warriors a ways back," Fargo said. "Someone did them in."

"You're not an Injun lover, are you?" Milton asked suspiciously.

"Because if you are, we'll have no truck with you," Rafer declared.

Fargo nodded at their horse string. "Did you kill them for their animals?"

"Not just for that, no," Alonzo said, and scratched a hairy ear. "We killed 'em mainly because they were redskins. Now we're bound for Denver."

"Then it's on to the mountains where we aim to strike it rich," Elias said.

Milton nodded. "Why, they say folks are pickin' the stuff right off the ground. Gold nuggets as big as your fist."

"Or maybe we'll find silver," Elias said excitedly. "We hear tell they've found veins of it as wide as a Conestoga."

"Can you imagine?" Milton said.

Fargo sipped and smiled and said, "Idiots could."

Their friendly smiles faded and Rafer growled, "What was that about idiots?"

"I've been to the Rockies more times than you have fingers and toes," Fargo said. "There's gold, and there's silver, but it's not lying on the ground and the veins are hard to find. If it was easy, every mother's son as stupid as you four would be rolling in money but most end up broke or dead or both."

"You just called us stupid," Milton said.

"What else would you call someone who shot two Indians for no reason?"

"Hold on now," Alonzo bristled. "They were red. What more reason does anyone need?"

"Were they out to lift your hair?"

"No, they was just ridin' along," Alonzo said. "They even acted friendly when we rode up but we didn't pay them no never mind and shot them down."

"Red curs," Rafer growled.

Alonzo nodded.

Milton showed most of his teeth in a happy grin and exclaimed, "They never knew what hit 'em."

"What about their women?" Fargo brought up. "What about their kids?"

Alonzo's dark eyes narrowed. "What the hell is wrong with you, mister? Are you white or what? Who cares if they had women or sprouts? They were *Injuns*. Dirty, filthy, stinkin' redskin Injuns."

"I was afraid that's how it was," Fargo said wearily. He sighed and set his cup on the ground so his hands were free for what came next.

"Why afraid?" Alonzo asked.

"Because I am sick to death of peckerwoods like you," Fargo told him. "Because now you have stepped in it and there's no way out."

"What the hell are you talkin' about?" Rafer demanded.

Fargo unfurled and stood with his right hand brushing his holster. "I'm saying you're the curs. And you're welcome to stand up and prove me wrong."

"You're proddin' us, is that it?" Alonzo said.

"He *is* an Injun lover," Milton said as if it astonished him.

"Well, I reckon we know what we have to do," Rafer remarked.

Alonzo nodded. "Mister, we thank you for showin' your hand. You could have just gunned the five of us in the middle of the night."

"Five?" Fargo said, and spiked with alarm.

"That's the other reason we shot those heathens," Alonzo

said. "One of us had his horse crippled by a fall and we needed an animal for him to ride." He smiled and looked past Fargo. "Ain't that right, Willard?"

"It sure as hell is," said a gruff voice behind Fargo even as a gun muzzle was jammed against the back of his head.

No other series packs this much heat!

THE TRAILSMAN

#340: HANNIBAL RISING

#341: SIERRA SIX-GUNS

#342: ROCKY MOUNTAIN REVENGE

#343: TEXAS HELLIONS

#344: SIX-GUN GALLOWS

#345: SOUTH PASS SNAKE PIT

#346: ARKANSAS AMBUSH

#347: DAKOTA DEATH TRAP

#348: BACKWOODS BRAWL

#349: NEW MEXICO GUN-DOWN

#350: HIGH COUNTRY HORROR

#351: TERROR TOWN

352: TEXAS TANGLE

#353: BITTERROOT BULLETS

#354: NEVADA NIGHT RIDERS

#355: TEXAS GUNRUNNERS

#356: GRIZZLY FURY

#357: STAGECOACH SIDEWINDERS

#358: SIX-GUN VENDETTA

#359: PLATTE RIVER GAUNTLET

#360: TEXAS LEAD SLINGERS

#361: UTAH DEADLY DOUBLE

#362: RANGE WAR

#363: DEATH DEVIL

Follow the trail of Penguin's Action Westerns at
penguin.com/actionwesterns

S310